W9-DJN-191

Voices Under the Window

Voices Under the Window

by
JOHN HEARNE

FABER AND FABER

3 Queen Square

London

First published in 1955
by Faber and Faber Limited
3 Queen Square, London W.C.1.
First published in this edition 1973
Printed in Great Britain by
Straker Brothers Ltd Whitstable
All rights reserved

ISBN 0 571 09985 8

In Memory

of

MAURICE VINCENT HEARNE

PART ONE: THE WOUND

The riot began two or three hours after dawn.

A crowd of unemployed men had waited for the Minister of Labour outside the House of Representatives since early morning. In a way they had been waiting for a number of years: waiting and looking for jobs they were promised at election time; waiting for food, for clothes, for a little money to feed the children their women had once a year, ten months after the last baby. They were very tired of waiting, and by this time, after all these years, they had become quite angry. So they had stayed where they were and kept looking up the road for the Minister's big grey Packard.

When he came and was stepping out of the clean car on to the dusty sidewalk they moved forward to him. They asked him about the work his party had promised at election time. "Plenty of work soon, boys," he had told them, "just be patient. Plenty of work soon. Lord, boys," he had said, "you don't think I've forgotten you!" Then he had gone inside the House, a black man like themselves but one with great powers of expression in words. He could say nothing and make it sound like a roll of drums. And at public meetings when he was speaking into the great, eye-shining spread of faces he could cry like a bereaved woman, the tears pouring down his broken, vein-ridged face as it showed alive and passionate in the yellow light from the huge kerosene flares on the platform.

The crowd of men had watched the Minister go into the House in his wonderfully tailored light brown tropicals and his fawn felt hat with the silken, curled brim. Three years before, when he had been a sideman on a truck, he had been very lean, but now he had begun to show the curve of good eating on his buttocks and in his big thighs.

When he had disappeared through the doors of the House one of the men sighed and said, "Oh to hell wid dem all, dem will never do nuttin' fe' we." Then he had stooped down and taken a large stone from the gutter and he had hurled it with great care and force through a window in the front of the House. The man beside him had, after this, taken a long clasp knife out of his pocket. It was a good knife and he had sharpened it till the blade was not much thicker than a nail file. It was the only thing he owned beside the half-shirt he wore and his trousers which he had stolen one night from a British sailor who lay drunk on the sidewalk next to the dock-entrance. The man with the knife plunged it into the sidewalls of the tyres on the Minister's car; walking round the car and doing the job with a deliberate, careful fury.

10

The Wound

After that when a large crowd had collected, and when the policeman who had tried to arrest the stone-thrower and the knifeman had been badly beaten, they had set off down the road. The men who had waited for the Minister were in the lead and those following them had become a mob. On the way downtown they did a lot of damage to windows and pulled the big gas drums which were used as garbage cans across the streets. And by the time they reached the centre of the city it was a full-sized riot and they were met by other mobs of people. Everyone had begun to shout by now and there were frequent screams, meaningless but electric and maddening. The whole city had been preparing for this for a long time. They had prepared for it without knowing what they were preparing for, and now the riot opened and blossomed with the sudden urgency of a night-bell and with the fury of a gas spray when you put the torch to it.

The big stores in the city centre had pulled down their folding steel shutters and in every office they were stuffing papers into full fire-proof safes. Some of the white and brown lawyers, office workers and clerks had managed to get out of the city to their bungalows near the foothills. They had driven fast through the mob which was not yet thick enough to stop them: each car full, with people sitting on one another's laps and with the windows rolled up. A few people had not been able to get out and sat in their offices, sweating in the airless rooms.

The Commissioner of Police, when he saw what was

11

about to happen, sent out the emergency signal and the English troops came down to join the police. They didn't go down into the centre of the city but set about sealing off the roads that led out to the suburbs. Later on, they knew, they could close in on the riot from all sides.

2

Mark Lattimer, the lawyer, with his friend Ted Burrow, and his mistress Brysie Dean, got caught in the riot in a place called Coronation Lane.

They had come down to this section of the city just after sunrise when the coconut fronds hung dead in the still air, before the land breeze changed to the sea breeze. They were there because Lattimer, who was also a politician, had known that something was going to happen but he had not realized it was going to happen so soon. He had come down to see some of the people in his own party before they went out to work or went off for the day looking for work. And driving through the grey morning, with the slime and gutter smell mingling with the rank odour from the houses where people slept fourteen in a room, he had realized that perhaps it was a mistake for one of his colour to be down here to-day. This morning, more than he could ever remember, he had felt the weight of the years' oppression and suffering.

All the time that he was talking to the people he

The Wound

had come to see Lattimer had an urgent, disquieting sense of danger. Then as they were leaving one house, going through the hot yard with the women quarrelling round the pipe and the men under the tree sharing one cigarette, he said suddenly to Ted and Brysie, "Come on, people. I don't like this at all. Something's going to start."

They followed him quickly and they all got into his Austin which was parked outside the yard. He let out the clutch and they felt the wheels slide, then grip, in the old slime of the gutter, and Mark Lattimer turned the car into the mesh of lanes that led into the city centre. It was now almost nine o'clock and the sky was clear and pale and raw with heat.

"What's happened, boy?" asked Ted. "What happened back there?"

"I don't know," Mark stated. "Something has been inside me all morning, telling me it was going to happen to-day. I think it's happening now. I'm almost sure it is."

A man came down the street on a bicycle. He was dressed in a neat suit of strong olive khaki and he was riding hard, bent low. When he was nearer they saw him wave his hand, flapping it vigorously. Mark put on the brake and kept the engine running.

He recognized the man as a carpenter who was a member of his party and who had done some work for him once in the election.

The man put his head in at the window. He was black and the sweat had run down his face making shiny streams of clearer black. They could smell him where he had sweated through his outer clothes.

"Lawd God, Mr. Lattimer, sah," he said, "I t'ink I did know it was your car. What you doin' down here to-day, sah? Dis is no place to-day for a fair man like you, or an Indian man like you, Mr. Burrow. Oh Jesus, sah, all hell pop loose up de town, dem is burnin' everyt'ing dat will burn and dem is gwine kill before long. Riot start, sah, I tell you, bad riot start to-day."

And he left them riding hard down the lane, with his coat blowing back.

There was no sound in the car for a second, except the noise of the engine, then Brysie said: "Jesus Christ, Mark, you were right after all."

Mark Lattimer started the car again and as they drove they could see the riot news begin to filter into the people and the first crowds beginning to form and the knots of men begin to leave the shade of the trees in the yard and gather in the heat of the yards. They could feel the ugliness of what was happening start to make itself felt and to grow and they knew that it was only the beginning.

As they turned at the end of the street Mark Lattimer said: "I suppose you know what sort of time we're in for if we get stopped." He looked at them sideways as he spoke, keeping his main eye on the road, swerving carefully round the thicker knots of people as they gathered. The gatherings had begun to stare at the car with hostility and purpose.

The Wound

When he looked at them Lattimer could see the start of fear on Ted's face and Brysie's. It had been there all along, and his words had brought it out spasmodically. But he knew they were afraid, the way the good ones were afraid.

"God!" said Brysie. "It all seems so sudden. You just can't believe it's really happening. I knew it had to happen and yet I feel empty and sick, as if I'd never expected it." She held Lattimer's arm very tightly, gripping him hard for a moment.

"Maybe they shouldn't do it," said Ted, slowly and bitterly. "Maybe this isn't the way to get things done. But perhaps when you've taken the beatings they've done for so long, this is the only way you can show you've still got a heart left."

Lattimer said nothing. He was driving with great care through the thickening crowds. But he thought of what Ted had just said. It was a remark beyond Ted's age or class or formal education. It was an instinct and love for the truth of things that he wished he could have had at Ted's age.

In Coronation Lane they had to stop the car. The whole street was filled with the mob from the houses, and more people were coming out of smaller side lanes and joining them. They were in a bad mood, but not killing mad yet. Not enough of them. What was going on up in the city would have to work a little further into them for that. They moved as they could up and down the streets, forming and breaking new groups every minute. There were three men at intervals along

15

the street who had upset the big ash cans and stood them upside-down. They were standing on them and each of the three was screaming out a speech. Every now and again a lot of the mob would rush forward suddenly to hear what one of them had to say. It was a reflex movement from the whole body of the people and there was no allowing for it or any calculation possible. It was a mineral process.

They were not yet very dangerous if you kept cool, Mark Lattimer knew that, but they were sullen and letting the misery and the hate in them come slowly to the froth and heat where they would want to do anything. They would not let the car pass even when he blew the horn, and when he looked into his mirror he saw they had closed in behind.

"Come on," he said to the others. "Let's walk. We might get away with it, but you'll have to look as if you expect to."

He opened the door on his left, leaning over Brysie to do it and she got out and he followed her. Ted opened the back door and they shut the doors again without bothering to roll up the windows. They stood there in the sun, blinking a little in the glare from the zinc roofs, with the gutter smell and the scent of rising hate around them and the stink of sweat from heated, badly nourished bodies.

"Now, look," Mark Lattimer told the two of them. "Walk cool and not too fast. About two streets up there's a man I know. He's a party member, at least he was. He might put us up."

The Wound

"O.K., boy," said Ted. "Let's go."

They set off up the sidewalk and they were only pushed a little by the crowd. Several times Mark could see that he was recognized. But there was a bleak frozen anger in the faces that knew him. It was an utter rejection of any advance that he might make. It was much worse than being not known. Halfway up they came opposite one of the speakers on the drum. He was a big man with the forearms that a dray driver develops pulling on the reins against big mules; his face was flat and very broad and he was screaming his speech. The crowd was making too much noise for Mark Lattimer to hear what he was saying.

As they got opposite the man there was one of the sudden mob rushes, closing in on the speaker on the drum. Mark felt himself carried forward and his shoes splash in the gutter; Brysie was holding on to his arm very tightly. Then they were out of the first heavy swell of the move and standing on the edge of the sidewalk with a small, temporary, clear patch of road between them and the people. It was then that Mark Lattimer first, and afterwards all of them, saw the little boy.

He was about four years old and had got into the middle of the crowd and when they moved forward he began to fall, slowly, on to his face. To Mark Lattimer the child, with his too round belly and his vest and no trousers, seemed to fall with ridiculous slowness; he seemed to take a long time reaching the ground. Then he saw he was being held up, squeezed by the muscle-taut, straining calves and knees of the people among whom he had been. Brysie felt Mark shake her hand loose and she saw him go in, crouching low, into the legs of the people, and she and Ted saw him wind an arm round the little boy's waist and pluck him out just as the movement of the legs would have tossed him to the road under the stamp of the broad feet.

He came back, grinning a little, with the child under his arm bawling like a goat. Mark put him down on the sidewalk right side up and leaned over to comfort him before the three of them moved on. Brysie and Ted began to walk the few paces that separated them from Mark. And a man came out of the crowd suddenly, a thin, good-looking, broad-cheeked mulatto, with his eyeballs as red as coals; he was carrying a heavy, soft-iron machete, the blade dark and smooth except for the edge which was bright silver, with the file scratches plain across it. He came up behind Mark and said, in a low, cold voice of remote madness, "Put him down, you white bitch." Then he chopped Mark with the expert, all wrist and forearm driving motion of a man who has cut bananas on a plantation or has killed the beef cattle as they come plunging and terrified out of the slip-gate on the cattle-pens.

3

The blow drove Mark Lattimer a few staggering feet to one side. They could hear him grunt and they saw his face twist suddenly over his shoulder, grimacing

and astounded. Then he fell over on his back, sprawling
in that wide-flung final way of a badly hurt man. The
man who had chopped him turned and vanished as he
touched the edge of the crowd; the child looked once
at Lattimer as the man lay and afterwards trotted
purposefully up the sidewalk. Ted and Brysie began
to go forward to Mark.

They were running but their movements were heavy
and desperate like people trying to climb quickly on
to a sloping beach against a strong backwash of waves
and the woman went past them and reached Lattimer
before they had covered half of the few yards. She was
a tall, strongly-built woman with the very straight
back and the wonderfully developed diaphragm of a
person who carries heavy baskets on her head. When
Ted and Brysie reached her she was already on her
hands and knees over Mark so that she was shielding
him in case the crowd surged back: crouched over him
with the front of her dress fallen away showing the
perfect, slightly elongated globes of her great, black
breasts. As Ted and Brysie dropped down beside her
she looked up and said, "Ah, tank God, missis. Him
belong to you, no? Tek him up to my room, him is
hurt bad. Oh God, but dem hurt him bad."

She lifted one hand and pointed it quickly across the
sidewalk, to a flight of concrete steps that led down
from a narrow-fronted house to the pitted, filthy sidewalk.

"Dat's my room dere," she said. "At de top of de
steps. Tek him up dere quick."

She squatted back on her heels, slipping a long rounded arm under Mark Lattimer's heels and Ted went to Mark Lattimer to gather him up under the armpits: then they rose and carried him, out of the heat and dust where he had bled on to the road, up the steps, staggering a little under the awkward weight of a big, unconscious man. They brought him into a little, dark room and laid him on a thin narrow bed with worn, carefully-washed sheets. Brysie followed them and tried not to look at the sudden, vivid splashes on the steps where Mark had bled. She could feel the pounding weight of her outraged heart and at the top of the steps she stopped to look at the people in the street below. Only a few had realized what had happened, and looking into their faces she saw no concern at all but only interest and hostility. A man laughed up at her with the hate and power in him making the laugh bitter and she turned quickly and went into the room.

He lay as they had put him in the bed; with the blood running out of his side and soaking brightly through the sheets. His eyes were closed and the nostrils were shiny white. To Brysie his strained, shallow breathing seemed the loudest, most unavoidable thing she had ever heard and she knew that she must be cooler and more efficient now than she had ever been before in her life; that now she had no time for any mistakes. Afterwards she could allow herself to go, all at once, into pieces, if she could not hold the pieces together.

The Wound

"Do you have another sheet?" she asked the woman.

The woman went to a cheap, thin-board dresser, with a blotched, badly-silvered mirror, that stood against the opposite wall. She pulled out the bottom drawer and reached inside and took out a folded-over, white, starched sheet that had a roughness of careful mending on the top fold. She handed this to Brysie, who took it quickly and flapped it so that it unfolded, stiff and clean and startlingly white in the little dark room. Brysie nicked the edge with her teeth and tore the sheet into the strips she wanted. Then she laid the strips on the bed and went over to the small table which, covered with green-squared oilcloth, stood in the far corner of the room. She took a large enamel jug of water from it and went back to the bed and with three strong, very gentle movements ripped Mark Lattimer's shirt away from his body and pushed back his jacket, exposing the purpling edges of the wound in his side, high up on the rib case, as it had cut through the prominent latissimus dorsal muscle. She poured the water over the wound till the bed was soaked above the first dark stain with a paler colour like mercurochrome. She made a thick pad of one strip of the sheet, pressing it over the wound, and told Ted to pass another strip over it and tie it hard across the chest on the other side. After that she rolled a bit of the sheet into a ball and tied it under the armpit as tight as she could to make a tourniquet. Then she took off Mark's shoes and lifted his feet a little to drag down the sheet on which he lay and pull it up again over him, and knew

21

that she had done everything she could do until the time they could get a doctor to him.

When she saw there was nothing else she could do she turned to the others. They were waiting for what she would say.

"Do you think there's any chance of an ambulance or a car coming in for him?" she asked Ted.

He shook his head.

"I don't think the ambulance would get through," he told her. "Not now. They'd have to come through the worst of it, and the streets are probably blocked."

"Then we'll have to get a party of policemen in," Brysie said. "They can come in on foot, with a stretcher."

"Yes, they might do that. Especially as it's Mark."

"Where's the nearest station from here?" she asked.

"'Bout a mile, missis. Maybe more," the woman said. "It's up toward de old Market."

"Ah yes," said Ted. "I remember." He began to go towards the door.

"Ted!" Brysie called out to him sharply. "Don't be a damn fool. How far do you expect to get?"

He came back from the door.

Brysie turned to the woman. "Are you going for us?" she asked.

"Yes, missis," the woman said. She was completely under the tremendous dominance Brysie had established in the room.

"You're sure you're going to do it for us? Just as I tell you?"

"Oh God, yes, missis. Nobody gwine trouble me."

"Then tell them up at the station that Mr. Lattimer is down here hurt badly. Tell them to come as soon as they can. All right?"

"Yes, missis."

"Then you better get going," said Brysie. The woman went without another word.

Ted opened the door for her and watched her go down the little steep flight of dirty steps, plump and with her big squarely-curved hips rising and falling alternately to the movements of her round, beautiful, straight legs. He shut the door again carefully, turning the cheap, soft-iron key in the lock. He looked across the room to where Brysie had sat down on the only chair the room had, which she had drawn up at the head of the bed. She was looking at her hands, which lay in her lap, black against the pale green of her shark-skin skirt; her body was slumped and broken as if she were taking a rest after enormous work. For a moment Ted saw her clearer and more vividly than he ever would again: the black and slim-boned face with the curved, Arab nose and the big, generous Negro mouth; the fine, curved body and the coarse, straightened, Negro hair fitting around the skull like a stiff helmet of lacquered, blue-black wire. He sat on the edge of the table.

"Brysie," he said. "It's going to be all right, you know. Mark is going to be all right."

"I hope so," said Brysie. "I want like hell to hope so."

4

Mark Lattimer opened his eyes a few minutes after
the woman who owned the room had gone.

He did not know at first who he was, or where. Then
he heard the mutter and the shuffle of the crowd below
and felt the pain in his side and he knew.

There was a calendar on the wall opposite his eyes:
it showed a long fat girl in beads, simpering over her
shoulder, and with a macaw clutched on to the stiff
forefinger of her right hand. He saw this and stared
at it a long time before he realized that Ted and
Brysie were in the room with him.

Close by him he saw the blur Brysie made in the
corner of his eye and he smelt her, the scent coming
to him of clothes and powder and the bitter-sweet profound odour that is so very old and which he had
always smelt on the women, and only on the women,
that he had loved.

"Brysie," he said, "give me a drink of water."

"Oh, Mark, Mark darling," said Brysie. And she
leant over quickly and put her arms with great gentle-
ness on either side of his head and took his face between her hands.

Ted brought the water in the jug, and while Brysie
raised Mark's head a little he put the edge to Mark's
lips. Mark swallowed deeply at first; then very easily
as the pain began to come; then finally not at all.

It came drawing through him, hard and unyielding,

24

the flesh curled about it unresistingly. The flesh shuddered heavily around the long, steady draw of the pain. It came still when he had told himself that he could not feel it any longer. And as it dragged through him it brought his death so close that he knew it. His death came so he could see it clinging at the end of a dark iron rod of pain; and as it disappeared through a great hole of agony he saw his death turn into a little, bright, malevolent figure that turned and leered at him before it disappeared at the end of the long, the endless, iron rod.

That's it, he told himself. That's it. It's come. I never knew it would come like that. But I always knew I'd know it when it came. Oh Jesus, Jesus, Jesus, I don't want to die now. Oh Jesus, I don't want to die when I'm loving Brysie and everything so much.

He let the fear pass through him as the pain had done. Then as everything went and left only Brysie and Ted and himself again he wondered how much of it he had shown.

He had shown his pain. His hand had held Brysie's so hard that he could feel her cold: and looking at their suddenly pinched, appalled faces he knew how much he had shown the agony. But he did not think he had shown his death. And he determined he would not show it before it came back so strong that they would see it leering up from his eyes and his skull. He remembered how the skull always showed through on a man just before death became certain. He had never lied to these people but he wanted to have them close to him before he died; before they knew about it. He wanted them as he had known them and he was going to lie to them now.

"It's all right," he said. "It's all right now. It hit me suddenly though, like feeling it all over again."

He smiled up at them from the bed.

Brysie said, "Oh, Mark, if you hadn't gone in after that damn kid."

"I couldn't help it," he told her. "He looked like a black version of my son. I just couldn't help it."

"Hero," said Ted.

Mark grinned at him.

"Remember that," he said, "and recommend me for some sort of medal as soon as we leave here."

He felt very tired but he would talk. It cost him a great deal but it was much better, among these people, to talk than to let the minutes go away in nothing. The tiredness was not yet important enough.

"Who chopped me?" he asked. "Did you know him? I never even saw the bastard's face."

"I don't know," said Ted. "I never saw him before. He probably didn't mean it though. Is that any comfort?"

"Not really," said Mark. "It will probably have to do, but it is not really any comfort at all. Why didn't he mean it?"

"He'd been smoking the stuff," Ted told him. "He was hopped to the brows with it . . . ganga. You should have seen his eyes. Pools of blood."

Mark listened to him and thought for a minute of

the man who had never seen him and whom he would never see. He thought of the way they had met and for how short a time.

"My God," he said. "My God!" Then after a while he added, "I suppose drugs move a man the way he's really been all his life. I'm just the sort of fair, almost white, that chap has wanted to kill all his life. He's hated me and been afraid of me more than anything. Just as I've hated him and been afraid of him and his colour more than anything else."

"That's pretty good," said Ted, "only you don't take drugs."

"Mark," Brysie said to him, "why do you always have to say things like that? You don't hate people because they're black. You don't hate people at all. You love me and I'm blacker than a lot of them out there."

She kissed him softly, and he could feel her sadness.

"I love you, Brysie," Mark said with great seriousness.

From the street there suddenly rose into the room a clamouring, deep roar of sound. It was lonely and a little mad; frightened, and full of hate raised to the place where it was ready to destroy. They listened to the sound grow and then subside shaking like a roll of thunder across the mountains. Out of the sound they heard the nerve-cracked voice of the speaker on the drum falling on the people like a whip. It was all as sad a thing as any of them had ever heard.

That's the sound, Mark said to himself, that's the

sound I've always heard. It's the music I've moved to for so long. Most of the time without even hearing it. Only the rhythm entered me waking and sleeping. The black people bellowing at me to get off their necks, and the whites, too, screaming nervously, not so often, more refined, whenever I came nearer than a certain limit. Maybe some day I could write a book and call it *The Diary of a Racial Climber*.

Then all at once he remembered he would never leave the room alive to write a book or to do anything again. And suddenly too he was a long way out of the room although he realized he must have been leaving it for a long time and he was back in what he was and the things he had done to make himself. So far back that when he saw himself he almost did not recognize who it was and the country was almost like a place he'd never been. . . .

. . . The gully where the children played came first of all out of the foothills. It came out of the green in a severe, dim yellow gash; straight and clean as it had eroded. Then it wound across the sloping plain to the sea.

In its plain tract it was broad and the floor was flat; the earth was dry, and baked grey and shiny, with wide cracks on the surface. A few tough, hard-green bushes that grew during every dry season when the gully wasn't in flood, dotted the bed. Along the banks were thick rows of fertile-looking trees and the grey-green, horny, long-thorned *macca*. On the far side was

28

the big stretch of open land with the tall pale Guinea grass waving and ruffling. On the near side were the backyards of the low-slung, cool bungalows where Mark and his friends lived.

The children were stalking for birds very carefully down one side of the gully. Mark was in the lead holding the heavy .22 B.S.A. air-rifle he had borrowed from his uncle. It was almost too heavy for him to hold properly and give it the rest you had to attain before aiming accurately. It was really beyond his years and strength, but he had it now because he had earned it. His uncle had never allowed him to fire it outside of the yard and only under supervision, but he had promised to lend it when Mark could aim it and hold the aim the way a man should with the gun he fires. For a while Mark had thought he would never be able to do this in the manner he knew he must. Not until he had read in a geographical magazine about the Himalayan porters.

The article had said that though these men were small and rather weak they had yet trained themselves to carry huge loads for incredible distances up almost perpendicular slopes.

Mark had told himself that if they could do it for one set of muscles so could he.

He went under the house where he lived which was raised off the ground on concrete blocks because it was in the tropics. There in the gritty, rat-smelling cool darkness he had found the length of old, heavy lead piping he had come to look for.

He took this out and for nearly three months prac-
tised raising it to his shoulder and sighting along it
as he would aim with a gun. When he got so that he
could hold it absolutely still for half a minute he tied
the flat irons the servants used to press clothes on to
the end. In a while after that he could hold the pipe
and the irons quite still and aim well.

The next afternoon at his uncle's place he found the
B.S.A. fitted him as if he had used it all his life. His
uncle hung old electric light bulbs from a long string
tied to a tree branch and then swung them. Mark
shattered twelve in a row, at thirty yards, only missing
the tenth with his first shot. By then his uncle had
used up all the old electric light bulbs he had.

"You can borrow the gun," he said, walking down
to Mark. "You can borrow the gun any time you like."
He didn't ask him how he had managed to hold it as
he had done.

"O.K.," said Mark. "I'll take it now. I want to go
after ground doves tomorrow."

"If you get enough," his uncle told him, "you might
bring me a couple. That is, of course, after you have
given your mother and father."

"All right," the boy said. "I'll bring you mine even
if I don't get enough. Thanks very much for lending
me the gun."

"Don't mention it," said his uncle. "I am glad to
lend it to someone who knows how to use it. Good
luck tomorrow."

He watched the boy go out of the garden with the

barrel of the rifle over his shoulder and his hand on the stock. He had no fear at all as to what the boy would do with this very powerful rifle. He would use it well; and he would love using it so much that he could never use it badly or idiotically, because that was the thing he had been taught to do. Watching him, the man wished he knew what it was had gone into the winning of it. He only knew it was something determined and handsome and carefully worked for.

Now, in the heat and the slightly sour, exciting smell of the gully dust, the boys watched carefully for the ground doves they had come down to shoot. They moved as softly as they could in their rubber-soled canvas shoes; the thin, sun-glossed bodies in the faded khaki shorts and well-mended boys' shirts, slightly crouching. In the lead Mark stopped and began to raise his rifle and the boys saw ahead the pair of plump coppery-green doves feeding on the gully floor in precise, rapid little pecks. Behind Mark they fanned out, lining up for the best shots. His best friend Lloyd Roberts, moving clumsily as usual with his knock-knees, stepped on a dry branch as he came into place at the end of the spread-out boys. Almost before the dry snap had died the doves were in rapid flight before them; skimming the ground, dipping and rising in staggering fussy flutters.

Mark could hear the twang and vibrating echo of the other air rifles around him. Then he had the rear bird in his sight and followed its dart to one side and allowed for the next spurt it would make, leading it a little, ahead and slightly above, and squeezed round the trigger, using the pressure of his contracting hand, and saw the bird dive into the ground tumbling lightly yet plumply in a brief, fine powder of dust.

There wasn't much doubt about who had shot the bird, because all had heard Mark's rifle after they had fired. There was no mistaking the deep, powerful vibration of his spring against the lighter tone of their smaller, boys' weapons. But all the same they went forward and picked up the bird, still warm and nervous with blood although it was quite dead. They dug carefully in the wound, just behind the neck, with the small blade of Lloyd Roberts' pen-knife which was the best knife the group owned. When they had dug out the slug and Lloyd held it wet and bloody in his palm they saw it was Mark's. The others, and Mark also before he got his uncle's rifle, all painted their slugs a different colour. They used very sticky house paint, putting a thin coat on the round pellets with fine brushes from their paint boxes. That way they avoided arguments when the rightful owner of a bird was in doubt. Most of the paint scraped off the pellets on their way out of the barrels, but there was generally enough left to decide accurately. With Mark using the B.S.A. he had not needed any paint on his slug. The big .22 took a different pellet from the others; a hollow thing with a rounded head, a narrow waist, and a flared tail to flight it well.

He took the bird and put it in the newspaper-lined satchel he had slung over his right shoulder.

The Wound

They shot well for the rest of the morning. Mark got three more; two doves which he killed on the ground and a nameless, dun-coloured bird which he killed on a branch above the gully and which he nearly lost in the bush around the tree. Of the others, everybody but Lloyd Roberts managed to get at least one bird, and three of them got ground-doves.

About one o'clock they were dusty and shiny where the sun had fried the sweat as soon as it came out on their faces. Everybody was feeling hungry, and they began to walk back home down the gully all at the same time when Mark said he was going home for lunch.

When they climbed out of the gully and got on to the heat-shimmering, soft tar of the road, they began to separate, dropping off into the various green-hedged gardens that stood trimly and secure about the cool, solid bungalows.

At the gate to the house where Mark lived, Lloyd Roberts stood with him for a minute.

"Well, I'll see you later on," Lloyd said.

"O.K." Mark told him. "I'll come over about four."

Lloyd began to move away, then he came back.

"That was a lovely shot," he said simply. "The first one. I wish I could shoot like that. My dad is always going on because I can't shoot."

"Oh, it's nothing really," Mark told him, shifting his feet a little, glowing with pleasure. "It's only because I practise and practise. Besides with a gun like this you can't help it. I'll tell you what I read the other day," he lowered his voice and let the importance of what he was going to say surround them, "I read in a magazine that these models were *hand-made*."

"Gosh!" said Lloyd, "your uncle must be a real sport to let you have a gun like that. Even for borrows."

Mark made a casual deprecating gesture that implied it was all in the family but that it was a pretty good family to be in.

When Lloyd left him he went into his front garden and up on to the verandah, which was shut in, protected and cool with the thick rice-and-peas vine and with the handsome cane furniture casually and carefully arranged along its length. He went in through the darkened cool drawing-room and dining-room where the dark glimmers of mahogany shone, and out on to the back verandah. Here it was light and hot with glare and smelled of the hot flat-irons on the coal pot and the scent of starched, freshly-pressed white cloth. The servants were working and laughing together as they worked: Alice was ironing the clothes; Lyn was squatted on a stool with a big earthenware bowl on her lap, picking rice, her skirt drawn up over the glossy black knees and tucked primly down between the big, round, shiny thighs. Dan, the garden-boy, was out under the big avocado tree cutting and joining a new length of rubber hose. Mark stood awhile and admired as he always did the way the man's huge, deceptively fluid muscles played along his shoulders and his back.

"Hi, sah," Alice said to him fondly. "You come home late to-day. Where you been?"

"Oh," he said, "I was down in the gully."

He leant the air-gun carefully in a corner and slung the satchel strap over his head.

"I went shooting," he told them and took the birds he had shot from the now damp and blood-stained newspaper. He laid them along the verandah rail. First the three ground doves, close together, then the other, unnamed bird a little way from them to show it wasn't of the same quality.

"Lawd, Missa Mark, but you is a shot. You gwine shoot crocodile next. Well, four bird, all one time."

Mark knew Alice was very proud of him. She had the same pride in doing a thing so well that you yourself could not do it better. It was one of the things he had learnt from her, although he did not yet know it, because she had been in his life from before he was born. He leant against the verandah post and prepared to enjoy her pleasure a little before he asked for his lunch.

"Missa Mark," Lyn joked him from the stool where she sat, looking up from the bowl of rice. "Missa Mark, you don't know, no, dat it's out of season fe' shootin' bird? Suppose de police catch you shootin' bird dis time of year. Dem lock you up, you know."

"Cho," said Mark, "they wouldn't trouble me."

"Oh yes, sah, dem will arrest you and lock you up."

"Not me," said Mark joking her back. "They don't trouble white people."

Something cold and bad came on to the verandah. It came, bringing the liveliness and friendly warmth to a sticky halt. It was more than being uncomfortable, it was something guilty and needless and wrong that he should not have said. He had spoilt what they all had because he had seriously meant his reply although it was only joking back at Lyn.

Blushing, he heard Alice stamp her iron heavily on the sheet she had spread out on the board. He saw Lyn look intently into her bowl of rice. Dan came over slowly to the steps, huge and supple and narrow-waisted in his torn vest and patched khaki trousers.

"Missa Mark," he said dryly from below, "*you* not white, you know."

All around him Mark could feel the unanimous hostility and the trouble he had started. Now he was alone and exposed and nowhere; he suddenly realized that he could call on no one to help him through this thing. He was very lonely, and he sensed, in a new, disturbing way, that he had sprung a trap on himself that would never quite let him go. What he was in for had too suddenly involved him for any hope of protection. He would have to go through with it to the end. And he would have to go through with it because he had never thought of himself as anything else but white, and the world he knew was only made for the values of being white.

"What do you mean?" he asked angrily and desperately. "I'm not black, I'm not brown. I'm white."

Dan looked up at him.

The Wound

"You not white," he said, "you is not a white man, Missa Mark."

"Then what am I?" Mark shouted angrily. "If I'm not white? Of course I'm white. Look at me." He held up his small, fair-skinned, sunburnt hand. He looked at the women and saw them look away. Terrified, now, and completely shaken he looked down at the black man.

"You not white, Missa Mark," Dan said quietly, and implacably. "I tell you dat. You is a brown man like your Daddy or your Mammy. Ask dem when dey come home. Don't say you is a white man, Missa Mark, because you ain't."

Mark was not frightened any more, although he was still lonely. More than anything else he was astonished and a little angry at this uncalculated, definite intrusion into the comfortable pattern he had thought was his life. Something he had was being carried and torn down so quickly and finally that he couldn't believe it.

"Look, Dan," he said, pointing at the creamy skin of his chest, showing the place where his clothes protected it from the sun. "Look at that. You going to tell me that's not white."

"But Missa Mark, you not white, sah. Why you don't listen? You is a brown man. How you can be white, sah?"

The two of them shouted a long time at each other. Then Dan went back to his hose, and Mark knew that no one could be so sure of himself as Dan was and not be right. He looked at the women and saw their faces full of troubled response.

He went into the house, and the whole day and everything was sad and troubled. Now, looking at his square, plump, rosy face in the mirror in his bedroom, and seeing the crisp, curling, brown hair his whole feeling for his life had become clouded and terribly confused, and he thought sadly of the boy who half an hour before had come into the house. . . .

5

The heat in the little room had become terrific now that the sun was well up the sky and shining straight down on the zinc. Brysie and Ted had begun to glisten although they wiped their faces often with handkerchiefs that had turned grey and wet.

It was a close, oven heat, smelling of cheap, uncured boards and the sour dust in the yard and the bodies close together in the street below.

Mark lay in the blood from his wound and sweated although he felt a little cold. All the cut nerves were throbbing and twitching and in the whole of his right side was a numbness that burned.

He turned his head slowly so that he could see Brysie and not forget anything about her face in the time he had left. And what had happened to him now, and all the things that he had made happen before, all the defeats he had known because he had failed to

38

meet the things a man had to meet, they were gone
for a moment because of Brysie and the way he had
managed to love her. For a minute holding her hand
as tightly as he could and looking at the well-known.
always new face above him he quite forgot he was
dying.

Brysie leaned over a little closer and looked at him,
then she turned to Ted.

"What's keeping those damned people?" she asked.

Mark could hear the fright sound harshly in her
voice and he sighed a little because the harshness destroyed what he had held so closely a minute before.

"It's all right, Brysie," he told her. "They'll be
quite a while coming. The streets must be in a hell of
a state. Besides, there were probably not enough of
them to send out."

"How are you?" asked Ted.

"Not too bad," Mark lied to him. "There's practic-
ally no pain and I feel quite comfortable, really, just
lying here."

"I'm glad about that," Brysie said. "Oh, God, but
I'm glad about that. I couldn't stand it if you were
in pain."

Mark smiled up at her and moved his hand slowly
along the back of hers.

"What's it like outside?" he asked Ted.

Ted went over to the window and standing against
the wall looked down into the street. He was there for
a while and Brysie got up and joined him. Then they
came back to Mark.

Brysie sat down again at the head of the bed and took Mark's hand. Ted lowered himself gently on to the foot of the bed and leaned his elbow on the rail. He looked at Mark steadily for a while without saying anything.

"All right," Mark asked him, "What's it like?"

"Bad," Ted said. "Going to get worse."

"Bad as that, eh?"

"Yes. It's like watching somebody shaking a bottle of aerated water before flinging it against a wall. They've stopped the speeches now. They're talking. You know—getting each other up."

"Yes, I know," said Mark. "That's the last stage but one. Before they break. They'd have set off by now, only they don't know what they're going to do. They missed the first 'bus not being uptown when the business started. The excitement got a little diluted by the time it reached down here."

"It's going to be one hell of a riot," Ted remarked. "They've been cooking it for a long time."

"I was only ever in one riot," said Mark. "That was back in 'thirty-eight. I was a boy then but I can remember hoping that nothing would ever make me as frightened as that again. Do you remember it?"

"I was up in the country," said Brysie. "The papers came, after the rumours. My father said that only godless people went in for riot. He was keeping a family of seven on one and a half acres of land but he hated the rioters as bad as if he had owned the whole parish. He was quite a conservative type, my old man."

"I bet he was," Mark said. "All the same it's better to feel that rioters are godless people than just to feel frightened about them. The way your old man felt, he may have been wrong but he was somewhere. Being just afraid you're so damn lonely almost anything is better. That's the one time you're quite alone."

Oh hell, he thought, now you're getting philosophical. The next thing, you stupid, careless bastard you, and you'll be thinking about sin. Well, why not? You know you're dying. You're doing the most private unshareable thing a man can do. So why not go the whole hog? Have a hearty breakfast. After all you're the condemned man in this little drama. So why not have a good chew in all this sin? Sin and death. Hand in hand. Down Lovers' Lane. A marriage has been arranged and will shortly take place in the beautiful church of all souls in life of sin and death. Oh God, that was a good one. Philosophical as dammit. Civilized. Didn't it have a fine bloody but unbowed flavour.

"You blasted hero," he said; then, aloud, "You fine, wee, cowering hero." And he began to laugh.

He laughed because he was, suddenly, so full of sadness and fear that his throat hurt with tears. The burning in his side was no longer numb. It was a fierce glow in all his body.

"Stop it, Mark," said Brysie, "stop it. Oh please, darling heart, stop it. Oh, please Mark, please. You'll hurt your side."

Mark went on laughing. Quietly and deeply, quite helpless, with his head bent back a little on the pillow.

41

And all at once, while he was laughing, and not expecting anything at all but being able to laugh, Margaret came back to him. She came so close that he could hear her voice through his own laughter. He could smell her across the sharp scent of the room's uncured wood and the warm oilcloth on the table. She was back with him. And with her was the way it had been that time up in Canada. The time he was eighteen and had left home to train for the war. . . .

. . . From the runway you could see out across the sound on to the grey sea. Behind the station, over the road, were the woods which climbed steeply so you couldn't see the farms lying just behind the ridge. In the distance were the big mountains. These were twenty miles away but they were so huge that they seemed to hang over the station. On a clear day you could see the snow on the tops smooth and thick but glittering in little splinters of ice when the sunlight lay across them.

It was the best country Mark Lattimer had been in since he left home. Except that it was cool it was something like his own country.

The land was green and deep with grass. Everywhere there were bright flowers: going out to the road in the evenings in the open transport the petals from the bushes would flutter thickly into the truck and you could smell them as they crushed beneath your shoes. What he liked best though were the mountains dominating everything. Always there, massive and enduring but always new and secret and beautiful.

You took off on the first leg of the long triangular training flight with the engines of the big bomber filling your ears with a roar of huge, fast, rhythmical sound. Not a steady drone as they said in books about flying, but a definite, very quick pulsation that was somehow alive. In a few minutes after you were in the air you had passed over the last clearing and the last small house. And then for as long as you could fly there was nothing but the hard, sharply-cut edges of the mountains and the green and yellow forest with the big patches of brown and tawny scrub and rock. In the hollows were the lakes with the bright loops of the rivers coming out of them among the scattered trees and rough grass. The whole land was crumpled in great folds, and the masses of clouds above the land followed the formation of the ground so that sometimes you seemed to be flying up in a canyon of grey cotton wool. At other times looking out of the turret you could see in the distance a huge waterfall of cloud steamily falling between piled masses of darker cloud.

On those afternoons when they weren't flying Mark Lattimer and David Lumsden, who was Mark's navigator, would go out to the road as soon as they could. They would go out, wearing the small cocky forage caps they weren't supposed to wear off the station, and with the buffed buttons winking on the new officers' uniforms they were just getting used to wearing.

Once out on the road they would walk down it half a mile to the house where Peter the bootlegger lived.

Peter was a retired sea-captain and he sold beer to his friends at very little above the legal market price.

Sitting in the kitchen of Peter's house, Mark Lattimer and David Lumsden would drink beer and listen to Peter talk for about an hour. He was an old man and could remember China in the days of the Boxer rebellion. His wife, who was crippled with arthritis, would lie on a long couch in the room next to the kitchen. The door between the rooms was open and every so often she would interrupt Peter to remind him of some point in his story he had forgotten or had remembered wrongly.

"No, no, darling," she would cry, "that wasn't the girl who the American oil-agent married. That was Sonia he married. That girl you're talking about, what was her name? I can't remember it either. Anyway she got syphilis from the Japanese who said he was in cotton."

Her whole life had been spent on the mean, seedy fringe of starvation. That was how her whole life had been since her parents brought her to Shanghai after the revolution in Russia. When Peter married her and brought her to Canada she had realized that nothing would ever persuade her to believe or count on her good luck. The other life was still the real one to her. This, after twenty years, was still the holiday.

After the beer, Mark and David would go out on the road again. In about twenty minutes they would pick up a car going into Vancouver.

Going down the road in those late afternoons, with

44

the light lying golden on the big, green, flowering land, Mark realized that this was one of the best things he would ever have. That this was one of the times and this was one of the places a man would have to keep and protect in himself; knowing them so well and feeling them so strongly that nothing would ever be able to spoil it or take it away.

When they got into Vancouver it was always grey with the mist coming in from the straits and rosy with the lights shining through the mist. They'd go to the officers' club and get four bottles of beer and sit down at the table in the corner opposite the staircase waiting for the girls to come in.

When they came they would all have some more beer and then they'd dance. Or sometimes they would go to the pictures or, as it was summer, into the park, and lying on the grass they would listen to the concert. Gwen with her head on David's shoulder because that was the way they liked it, and he lying out beside Margaret so they touched from the ribs down to the ankles, holding hands very tightly, looking up at the pale sky of just before night and losing the day and themselves in the music.

Afterwards, when they had eaten, they would go to the Belman, which was one of the hotels where you could take a girl. There in the darkness with only the intermittent orange flash of a neon sign across the street Mark and Margaret would make love. Sometimes he would leave the light on so he could see the very white, cleft, strangely rounded body reaching out for him eagerly, drawing him to her with welcoming, gentle hands.

One night it was like nothing he had ever dreamed of, or read about, or heard. It was nothing that he could have imagined. Afterwards, it was like coming back from a long dead sleep in which you had been able to move and see and feel harder and deeper than you could do when you were awake. Lying there beside her so that her fair hair brushed his forehead, Mark could feel the world in which he lived, and time itself, seeping into his body like a blood transfusion.

She turned her head on the pillow so that their noses almost touched and their eyes could see nothing else but into each other's eyes.

"Do you know what?" Margaret asked.

"No," Mark said. It was a pleasant effort to speak.

"I feel so wonderful," she said. "It's so . . . comforting to lie with my head on your pillow and my hand in yours. Hug me, Mark, please."

He held her, then, very close and warm beside him, with her head on his shoulder and both his arms around her.

"I wish I could tell you how I feel," she said. "It feels so protected and happy."

"I know," said Mark. "But don't talk about it too much. Just feel it. If you talk about it too much you won't have it any more."

"Oh Mark darling, let me talk about it just a little. It won't spoil it for me."

"All right," Mark said, smiling. "Talk about it if you want to." He gave a sudden tight hug, so that she gasped. "Women seem to get more out of this than men. I don't think it's fair, do you?"

She laughed and lazily kicked her leg into the air pointing the foot and squinting along the toes. Mark watched the thick, round, muscle-taut thigh and ran his hand lightly along the smooth ribs of her deep, powerful body. She closed her hand over his tenderly and lifted it to her lips and kissed the palm softly.

"Do you think it's fair," Margaret asked him, "that they should stop the world just for the two of us?"

"No. You bet it isn't. It isn't democratic."

"You think other people feel like this?"

"A few. A few who lead good pure lives, like us."

"I wouldn't like my mother to hear about this sort of good, pure life."

"No," Mark agreed. "She mightn't understand. It's a good thing you are away from home."

She turned suddenly and hugged him, pressing him close to her.

"Oh Mark," she said, "we're so lucky. Darling, darling, aren't we lucky? Meeting like this, when we didn't have to. We could so easily not have met, darling."

He raised himself on one elbow looking down at her, at the strong curve of her small nose and the closely-cut fair hair ruffling out on the pillow, at the broadly-set dark eyes and the taut skin over her broad jaws. He ran his finger tip over the edges of her very wide

firmly-fleshed lips from which he had kissed the lip-
stick so that it was the pink of its own colour streaked
with scarlet.

"Loveliness," he said. "My own lovely loveliness."

All that summer and into early autumn the crews
were out on the coast. Towards the end of training
they began to increase the flying and by the last few
weeks they were only on the ground enough for theory
and to sleep. Of the ten crews who had begun the
course four had not finished. Two came down in the
mountains and they never found one of them. Another
went into the sea and though the big, long-range
Catalinas located the raft with four of the men aboard
they were dead from exposure. The last crew was blown
up one night when the oxygen tanks along the waist
exploded. The plane at the time of the explosion was
going along about a mile behind the one in which
Mark was rear-gunner. He saw it disintegrate lazily
with a slow incredible violence and then the bursting
quick flame against the grey clouds. Then there was
nothing but trying to believe what he had seen and
finding it all slightly remote and a little unreal from
what, a second before, they had all been doing together.

Even when they got down and were standing around
in the mess talking about it the whole thing seemed
unconnected with the real life of eating and drinking
and walking around together. Any minute he expected
to see the men who had died in the explosion alive
and talking. Not dramatically but in the most ordinary

way, standing in the mess and talking as they had been
for the past three months.

After they had finished training everybody was
given two weeks' leave.

Mark and David Lumsden took Gwen and Margaret
into the mountains.

It was quite a good party that went. Besides the
four of them there were three other couples with whom
they had been friendly all the summer.

They set off one morning with the Indian summer
mist still hanging over the woods and the fields. They
waited in the field at the far side of the road with two
couples standing on the bank and thumbing the cars
as they came along going up the valley. As one couple
got a lift another would come out. It was a good time
of the year with the woods crimson and purple and full
of yellow burning deeply on the leaves. The sky was
very clear and when it got well into morning it was
hot and dry.

They all met at Massachusetts Ferry about a hundred miles up at the head of the great fruit valley.

The other three men were civilians who worked in
one of the war factories down in Vancouver. They
were older than Mark and David but they had been
good friends to the two. The girls were about the age
of Margaret and Gwen and worked, like them, in
offices. Everybody was happy and warm and full
of the sheer, child-like exhilaration that you get at
the start of a good holiday. At the Ferry, they spent
the night in the hotel drinking beer until early in

the morning and laughing very easily at simple jokes.

In the morning they took the big, folded-up haversacks out of the suitcases and put on their walking
clothes. Then they went down into the little town and
bought quantities of bacon and beans and flour, putting them into the haversacks. One of the men knew
a bootlegger in the town and they went along to him.
He was still sleeping so they had to go round to the
back and knock on his kitchen window until he came
out tousled and gummy-eyed, in his dressing-gown.
They bought a dozen fifths of whisky from him and
then they went out of the town, with the haversack
straps cutting pleasantly into their shoulders, and then
across the wooden bridge over the green river into the
woods on the other side.

The trail that led to the place they were going was
narrow and at first it led up over a broad ridge. Going
up the trail they had to spread out in Indian file.
Mark kept looking into the woods on either side, to the
crimson of the sumac and the purple from the maple
glowing out of the pale yellow of the sunlight and with
everything less hot and fierce because of the clear
dominant light from the sky. When they got to risings
in the ground and he could look out between the tops
of the trees there were the snowy mountains hard and
clear against the sky with many-splintered, glittering
ice wrapped around each peak.

Out on the top of the ridge the wind blew thin and
cool from the peaks and the woods had thinned out so
they were among the pines, with the tawny scrub and

The Wound

the brown rock falling gradually before them to where
the thick crimson and purple trees began again. In
the distance, hazy with the heat, was the river where
they were going to camp.

When they had put up the two-man pup tents they
had hired in Vancouver the night was already closing in.

Mark wondered if there ever would be, again, a time
and a place like this. Whether, wherever he went again
and whatever he did, he would always have this just
as it was, with the dark bars of night coming across
the orange and green sky and the tents, with the lan-
terns in them shining through the canvas, standing on
the rough sweet-smelling grass of the meadow that
sloped down to the edge of the river.

At this place where they stayed the trail into the
deep mountains crossed by some big shallows. Here,
the water ran clear green and flashing frothy white
over the black granite rocks. On the other side were
rough, solitary standing firs.

The three civilians and the girls with them did a lot
of walking during the days. They went into the country
across the river or tried for trout in the pools up
stream.

Mark and David stayed mostly near to the tents
with Margaret and Gwen. They did a lot of sleeping,
and lounged on the grass talking things that sometimes were of great importance.

Just below the shallows where the river rushed over
the rocks there was a pool. It was cold and a deep
steel-blue in colour. The four of them, when the others

had gone walking and fishing, used to swim in the pool. They would strip off their clothes and run over the grass into the shallow rushing river at the end of the rapids, then dive off clear into the deep water. The water was very cold, but when you came out and someone towelled you down hard you could lie on the big, flat-topped rock above the pool while the sun baked the chill out of you slowly and gently.

Sometimes when they had lain in the sun for a long time and had slept a little, touching all along their lengths, the two couples would turn at the same time and make love. And afterwards there was no embarrassment and no shame.

In the evening, the others returned and after the meal they would sit around the fire on the grass and play poker and drink the whisky and talk. And sometimes there was singing.

After the trip was over, coming down from Massachusetts Ferry, they took two days to reach Vancouver. That was because they were passing through the orchard country and the people sold them huge baskets of fruit for next to nothing.

Sitting on the banks they let the cars pass; with the tart, exciting smell of hot tar coming off the road.

They sat under the trees and devoured uncounted pounds of huge, purple plums, great silvery gold pears and the fat royal cherries that had ripened all summer in the heat of the valley. It made them all a little drunk because they were autumn fruit and bursting ripe.

The Wound

Margaret liked the plums better than anything else and eating them the juice ran down her chin and over the front of her shirt.

"I must look awful," she said. "Do you think it will wash out?"

Rolling her big eyes she leaned against Mark, eager, breathing warmly and quickly, staining his cheek and shirt with the juice that was still wet on her.

"You look fine," he told her. "You look brown and fat and wonderful. And even if you're a dirty girl I love you truly. I'll always love you, my only love," he said, "I'll love you forever."

And afterwards. After that last night in the old Belman Hotel. And how she was the next morning when she came down to the train he was going to cross Canada on before he went to England. And the letters that went back and forth. The loving her and missing her so enormously that sometimes, especially at night, you wondered how you were going to get through the next stretch before you had some contact with her even if it was only by letter.

Mark remembered these things. And he remembered the gradual progression to the time where the letters did not mean so much. It must have happened more quickly that he thought because it was before the baby was born, when they could have still married by proxy; and the ways in which he did not get around to marrying her, with the death sentence of involving himself too much hanging across his days; and the way her letters went, not believing, then not wanting to believe what he was doing to her, and then the last letter, the letter before that last bitter one which said the baby was born dead, the one with all the things he knew about himself and what he had done but were there staring up at him perpetually from a letter. And he knew that he would never, as long as he could live, get out from under the thing he had done and the way he had failed.

PART TWO:
WARRIORS' CHORUS

1

He seemed to come back to the room very slowly. First there was the girl and the macaw in the picture on the wall opposite the bed, fixed and lurid. It had the horrible, exhausting rigidity of a really bad work of art. Then there was the stale smell of uncured wood, and the chemical smell of the oilcloth on the table. And after these, there was the glare at the window, from the sun outside writhing in a cloudless sky on to unshaded streets and zinc roofs. And in the heat he could smell the rancid, dusty-sour odour of the people in the street and hear the rise and fall of the voices.

Finally he saw Brysie and Ted. Both faces were stony and a little desperate with worry and helplessness.

"I'm sorry," he said, "I must have gone off the deep end there for a bit. Don't know why I did. Nerves, I suppose. Getting hurt must have cut all the nerves I have got screwed up too tight these last few months."

He was weaker than he had ever felt and the pain

had become a huge weight that he could scarcely carry alone. A big, red-hot mass that rested on the side where he had been cut but which spread from there over the whole of him.

Brysie smiled uncertainly. He could feel her hand on his relax a little its fast, involuntary squeeze. And Ted became a little less tensed at the foot of the bed. Mark knew he must have shown more confidence and given more reassurance than he felt. Well, he told himself, that's one of the things you learn from being an officer. It almost comes with the uniform. I thought I'd forgotten how to do it.

"Mark darling," said Brysie with great tenderness, bending over him. "When we get you out of here, and you're better, I'm going to see that you rest and rest, till you look like the advertisement for a laxative."

They all laughed at that. They laughed very heartily at that because it was around the bed of a sick and badly hurt man and everything simple is easier to do and seems much more important in those circumstances. Mark laughed too, although it hurt him so badly that he started to cough halfway through and had to stop, breathing very deeply to control his laughter. He looked round for something to say. Wanting this sort of moment to go on as long as it could.

"That picture," he said, pointing at it on the wall nearest the foot of the bed. "Reminds me of all our leading politicians."

"O.K.," said Ted, after he had turned his head and looked at it. "O.K. I'll admit you have a subtle, complex mind and I'm really just a peasant with shoes. But how the hell does it remind you of them?"

"It's so goddam bright," Mark told him. "There's such a lovely lot of colours all put together and they add up to nothing. They add up to just nothing. It really is very symbolic if you'd only see it."

And easy there, boy, he told himself. Now you're getting serious again. All worked up and serious. Whatever you do don't get worked up and don't try to be profound.

"Darling," said Brysie, "I don't want to spoil this, but don't you think you'd better stop talking? I don't think it's doing you any good and besides, we might start to laughing again. We always do, the three of us, when we're talking. You know that."

"Yes," said Mark. "That's a habit we got into. It is very frivolous, but there it is. We always seem to find something amusing to put into our talk. Amusing to us, I mean. To others, our jokes are no doubt abysmal."

"I guess we're just heartless," Ted told him. "I don't think our energies are really in the struggle."

He grinned from the foot of the bed and Mark saw again how Indian he looked. The taut, very dark, sunglazed skin stretching tightly over the broad mongolian cheeks and the dead straight, blue-black hair falling down one side of his forehead.

"You goddam image, you." said Mark. "You cigar-store statue. You look like Sitting Bull in a good humour."

"What sort of good humour?" asked Ted.

"Oh, like when he'd just scalped Custer or something."

They looked at each other, and Ted came up to where Brysie sat beside the bed. He reached down and took Mark's hand with a pretended roughness that was almost gentler than Brysie's touch. For a moment, the two men gazed at each other with an urgency that acknowledged the situation and yet hallowed it with love.

"You fool," said Ted, and went back to his chair.

Brysie looked at Ted, then slowly she turned and looked at Mark. And for a minute she looked from one man to the other. Her eyes were shining with tears that did not fall.

"Ted," said Mark slowly.

"Yes."

"Don't take me too seriously about that picture, eh?"

"I know," said Ted. "It's just the way you talk."

"Not always," Mark said. "Sometimes, a lot of the times, I believe it. It isn't all joking with me."

"Because it's true sometimes," Ted replied. "You know that. A lot of them, on our side of the House as well as theirs, are just like that picture."

"Yes," Mark told him, "but that isn't the whole of it. It isn't even, really, an important part. What matters is the work, and the truth of the work, even when it's done by little, sad, selfish people."

"You have to learn to recognize those people

though," Ted answered. "It's so easy for them to cash in on a time like this, to shine because of it."

"It always happens," Mark said. "It always happens in the easy time when you only have to criticize and prepare the ground. This is the good time for any party, Ted, when all the power and all the respectable people are against you and only the poor speak for you."

"And after that?" Ted asked him.

Mark waited, and he let what he wanted to say form itself slowly, piece by piece, across his mind. Always, the marriage and issue of things into words had been of great importance in his life. Part of life itself, even, in a definite magical fashion. The words became things, almost beings, in which were carried what had happened, what was, and what would be. They were the only form of life he knew of which existed in so many worlds, and were used by so many worlds, simultaneously. To him, it was always marvellous.

He lay back and watched Ted. He hardly felt the room, the heat, his wound: he was scarcely aware of Brysie's thin hand on his, nor of the grotesque, blood-stained riot in this city which was so much more to him than any other city. He only saw Ted, who leaned forward in his chair with that eager, reaching-out look: a look that was at the same time very young and wonderfully sure.

"And after that," said Mark, "it's trying to do a lot of things you can never finish. One man in his one life can never do it. But if you use yourself a little more than is rationally possible, that's enough. And to do it you have to give up everything that makes you a separate person. Making love, perhaps, if you're lucky, and eating, are all you can afford. All the rest of you has to be given and poured into the people and their world. You don't speak for them and work for them, but because of them. And the hardest part of the work you have to do is knowing when it's one million separate voices speaking or the one, unanimous voice. And to do the work faithfully you have to kill a little of yourself every day, till it's only the work and your faith that's left."

He looked at Ted as if asking permission to continue. He felt strangely shy of the point to which he had got. And he had only said it because he had so little time left in which to say this, or anything. And because he knew Ted would use it, and later make it much better than he.

"Don't get frightened," he said, "because of the things you might have to destroy. They're worth a lot and you can never put them back, but if you have faith in how much men have left in them to create then you needn't get frightened at all. It's not us who invented that faith; it's all the people and all their suffering that gave it us and made us one of them. And sometime, I don't know when, the people and the suffering and the faith and the work are going to come together and make a world as beautiful and valuable as . . . as . . ."

He waved his hand and lay very still, with his face pale and glazed as wax. He had tried too hard and his

bones felt as if they were pressing gently but inexor-
ably through the skin of his skull.

"Mark," said Brysie, "please don't talk so much.
Ted, please don't make him talk. It's bad for him. I
know it. Oh, why don't those damn policemen come
down from the station?"

Mark was not sorry to stop talking. What he had
been saying was one of the things he had learnt late
and one of the points by which he had tried to live
since he learnt it. And talking about it embarrassed
him. It was something you had to learn and make a
part of you after you have learned it, and then it did
whatever good it could do. To talk of it further brought
you to the edge of a dark, incomprehensible abyss of
the future where your words were useless. Now, there
was only the work that must be done. This was a
knowledge, and questioning only lost it.

He lay back and wished the bed were much deeper
so that he could sink further and further into it.
Sinking. With the bed closing over him, and the darkness making him forget how tired he was.

It was then that they heard the crowd below the
window go suddenly into madness. For a while now
they had been so quiet that you might almost have
forgotten them. If it had not been for the restless, eager
stamping of the feet and the menacing emptiness of
the voice that came up you might easily have forgotten
the danger. Then, in one instant, the to and fro stamp
became a rush and the rush mingled with a quavering
howl and there was a huge-voiced man somewhere at

the head of the mob screaming, "Kill dem! Kill dem! Kill dem!" And then they were gone out at the head of the lane leaving a sort of dripping, slow echo in a big silence.

The power of it brought Ted and Brysie to the window before the front of the mob were out of the lane. Mark was half-leaning on his elbow in the damp, red-stained sheets. And all their faces had that frozen, outraged expression you can see on a boxer's face at the precise instant he has been hit a tremendous blow.

"Oh God!" said Mark. Almost talking to himself. Not really saying it to them. "So that's what it sounds like. I'd forgotten. But that's what it sounded like the time I heard it when I was a boy. I'd forgotten, but I remember it now."

2

Ted came back from the window. Brysie followed him. She looked at the sheet where it was exposed as Mark had lifted himself and raised the coverlet. She tried to control her face and sat down again taking Mark's hand. Ted stood looking down at Mark.

"I think now they're gone I'll go and dig up something to get you out of here," he said.

"No Ted, no," Mark said urgently. He raised himself a little further from the pillow. "Listen to me, Ted, listen, man, let me tell you about riots. They never move to a centre; that's why they're so bloody. Only revolutions do that. Riots cross and weave a city like a crazy sort of folk-dance. You go out of here and the first thing you know you'll get tangled up with twenty or maybe a hundred and twenty men going someplace with broken bottles and cutlasses. They won't know where you're going, or why, but they're just waiting for a brown man like you. You ever seen a man after the boys have given it to him with broken bottles? I have, and I don't want it to happen to you. I don't want that it might ever happen to you. So stay where you are, for Christ's sake, Ted, stay where you are."

He began to get excited, then, and tried to get out of the bed. Brysie and Ted had to calm him down. And eventually, when he knew that Ted was not going to go but wait there until the woman had brought in somebody that could get him out, he lay quiet. He was sweating; the pain had become a thing inside him that was writhing like the sun, and now that he was sure about Ted he suddenly became detached from the room and the people in it.

It was a steady veering of his mind, and it came like being drunk and seeing yourself reeling. The steady part of you outside it all not because you wished it there but because you could not control it.

He was aware of his pain, wishing he did not have it: but that for now was not important. He could almost, again, see his death and for the first time since he had known it he was not afraid.

What he was aware of now was the pattern behind

these painful, unimportant things. He could see the pattern he had made and for a minute he could almost tie it to the things he was now on the bed. For a little while, lying there, he almost had it. Then the secret thread that would have led him through to what had happened was gone, and he knew he would never find it again. That he would only see the pattern: the way it had been and the things he had done. . . .

3

It was the summer before the war ended and he was outside the hangar waiting for David Lumsden's plane to come down.

Half an hour before he had landed. They had been on a very successful strike deep into Europe, beyond Germany, with the Americans. There had been a lot of planes and none of them in his section of the raid had been lost. Coming back, when they were over England, it had been pretty good, with everybody happy and the tension gone.

When the big American Liberators had peeled off to their station there had been a lot of back-chat and joking over the intercom.

"Goodbye, you old Yankee son of a bitch. Hope you've learnt something to-day."

And he could hear the muffled crackling as the voices came back from the turning away planes.

"Don't worry to thank us, Limeys. We'd like to help

you any time. Just call on us. We got plenty of planes."

This had gone on till the Wing Commander in the lead plane up in front had barked through for them to stop playing silly buggers for Christ's sake and act like decent airmen if they could.

Back at the station when they came in, rolling slowly up the length of the tarmac with the yellow fire tender in front and to one side, it was like it was every time you came down.

He had waited for the last, stepped-up roar from the engines and had felt the drag of the wheels across the tarmac and the bump as they went into the grass at the side of the runway. After that he had climbed out, swinging his parachute, and feeling stiff and bulky in his harness, with the ground strangely solid under his boots after eight hours in the air.

In the summer it was very hot even in the late evening and he had been sweating by the time he had walked over to the hangar and had given in his parachute. Then he had got his tea and gone over to the table where Intelligence asked you what it had been like. He had told them how many enemy planes he had seen and what the flak had been like and anything else the enemy had done or might be doing. It was nothing much by itself, but there were people who did nothing else but add what you had seen to something someone else had seen and made a pattern out of it that must have been often valuable. He knew this because he was now on the winning side of a war and nothing had hurt him yet and he only had five more trips like the one he had just done before they took him off.

One thing about talking at the Intelligence table was the way the raid came back to you in a cool pattern. You could see how it was from the time you left the warmth and food smell of the Mess and got into the truck to drive up out of the scattered wood in the hollow where the Mess hut was. You could remember in a detached way that dominated the whole experience how afraid and knotted you felt in your stomach as you heard the big shocking roar of the engines while the plane went down the runway. Then the leaping, tree-blurred, ground-falling-away rush and, almost immediately, the houses in the village under you, still close enough to make out the curtains in the windows. Then the whole land below becoming more remote and blurred, with the colours leaping out of the contours startlingly plain and the cold coming into the turret as you looked carefully at the four guns you were responsible for.

At the rendezvous you circled and then aligned in formation. You were high up by this time and the other planes in the raid kept coming up against the huge pale sky. They came up with deceptive slowness, hardly seeming to move at all, but swelling rapidly and every so often surprisingly closer to you, rising and falling lazily in your vision. All the way across England new planes would join them and by the time they were over the coast he would be able to see the

great stretches of dark cross-shapes against the sky
for miles.

That way they would go over till they heard the
whipping cracks of the anti-aircraft shells and saw
the oily, dark soot-blossoms of smoke as the shells
burst. Then over the target, already burning and half-
clouded by smoke, you would peel off for the run,
coming in through the clusters of flak and waiting for
the final run which had to be steady and left you
exposed and easy for the gunners below.

After Intelligence had finished with him, this
evening, he had taken a chair out of the flight room
in the hangar and propped it against the wall outside,
and sat in it to wait for David's plane.

He and David no longer flew together because three
members of their old crew had fallen sick and the rest
of them had had to join new crews. But the friendship
with David and David's family was still one of the
best things that had happened to him, in this war.
Being liked by someone like David and David's mother
and father gave him back a little of the thing he had
lost when he deserted Margaret.

He was sitting there against the wall, his feet in the
heavy flying boots propped up against the rungs of the
chair, when Tommy Hales, the Senior Intelligence
Officer, came to the doorway.

"Hello, Mark," he said. "You still here?"

"Yes," Mark told him. "I'm waiting for David. He
should have been in by now."

"They got hit," Hales said. "They picked up a bit

in the port engine on the way out. They just got through to us about it. They're all right but they'll be slow."

"That's all right," Mark said. "I'll wait awhile. It's a nice evening."

He accepted the news of David's plane without any surprise. Being hit was one of a number of things that you expected to happen to you every time you went up. You were relieved when they didn't and counted off another time to the time when you wouldn't have to expect them, but you were not surprised when they occurred. And you never tried to forget them the way the war correspondents imagined you were doing when they saw you drinking in the Mess. Whatever you tried to forget in the war, being hurt or being killed wasn't in it. Those things were with you all the time and so long as they did not begin to worry you too much you were all right.

"This is a lovely place to fight a war from," Mark told Hales, looking out across the big, green gentle folds of the country in which they were. "There's a line of trees at the edge of the aerodrome there against the sky that looks like a painting by one of the big Dutch boys."

"What do you know about Dutch masters, you ignorant colonial?" asked Hales, grinning down at him. "I bet you never saw a Dutch master in your life."

"The trouble with you bloody English," Mark said, "is that you don't have fine sensitive souls, like me.

68

And you can fight your own war the next time, let me tell you."

It was then that the sergeant from Intelligence came to the door with a worried face and gave Hales the message about David's plane and that the fire tender and the ambulance went out quickly on to the runway from before the hangar, the crews still scrambling into position; and almost immediately afterwards Mark could hear the sound of the plane coming in badly and falteringly.

It came in flat as a plank, falling suddenly out of the sky just above the sweep of tall, plumed trees at the edge of the aerodrome. It went straight into the grass at the top of the runway. Almost immediately it was burning fiercely. By this time the fire-tender and the ambulance were going up the runway very fast. Mark was running up from the hangar and when Hales drove past him in the jeep he hopped on to the side as it went by without knowing how he did it. Halfway up the runway the gas tanks blew up and a huge breath of scorched air rolled down the runway to them. The ambulance and fire tender kept straight on with spurts of the burning petrol falling on the tarmac around them. Nobody thought there was going to be much to do when they got to the white-blazing, shimmering skeleton of the plane.

By this time Mark had twisted into the seat beside Hales, who had his foot right down on the board. The fire-tender and the ambulance were side by side and seemed to go very slowly on the huge, naked, dark

surface of the tremendously long runway. The jeep
had almost caught up with them. Mark was thinking
nothing at all, with the surprise and shock still like a
leaden ball in his stomach.

When they were almost up to the two vehicles ahead
they saw the ambulance rake off the runway on to the
grass where the big bomber had churned up a wide
muddy swathe as it had bellied in. Somehow Calvert,
the wireless operator, had been flung clear before it
caught fire. He was on his knees where he had fallen.
His face was scraped clean, showing the white bone
streaked with red. His nose was a large squash of
black and his arms stuck out from the elbows at two
queer angles. As they came up Mark could see there
was not much left of his scalp. He was quite conscious
and kept saying in a whisper of unbelieving pain,
"Jesus! Jesus! Jesus!" His voice was too thick with
agony to carry very far. The men from the ambulance
gave him the morphia and he went under very quickly.

Afterwards, when it was quite dark, and they had
taken what was left out of the bomber, Mark and Hales
drove off to the Mess.

"I'm sorry," said Hales. "That was really a filthy
do."

"Yes," said Mark. "I guess it was. I wonder what
happened?"

"I can't imagine," Hales replied. "Not my pigeon
anyway. Engineering wallahs will have to decide that,
if they can. There isn't much left."

"It might have been anything," said Mark. "It

might have been any one of a number of things. You can't possibly keep your mind on all the things that can go wrong. Not at that speed. We ought to fly slower, or evolve a species who can match the odds."

"War is very complicated nowadays," Hales agreed. "Everything is very complicated nowadays. Especially the people. Do you know that you are a much more complicated young man than I was at your age? Only death remains just the same. There is just no complicated way of dying. There are plenty of complicated ways of killing, but dying is always just the same. I wonder science has let it alone. If I was a scientist I wouldn't let a little thing like death fox me, I'd make that complicated too."

Mark looked at Hales, at the big, hatchet-fashioned face he could just distinguish in the green dim glow of the dash board. He saw the long, ragged, greyish-white scar running up beside the nose over the left eye, then coming out of the patch and digging across the forehead like a dry river valley, with lots of little tributary scar tissues, before it disappeared under the cap. That was a long time ago, in another war, thought Mark, and it must have hurt a hell of a lot. It couldn't have been almost dying and seeing the men around him die, because it still worries him. And when you've been in it you stop worrying about dying afterwards, when it's over. But if you've been hurt really badly, if you've been hurt so that you go quite clean bloody well out of yourself, you always remember that. And you always worry and fret about it. It's something you

71

lose with the blood and you never get it back in the transfusion.

"Anyway," said Mark, "it must have been over quite quickly. I don't think they felt much."

"Yes," said Hales. "That's right. They didn't feel much. I don't think they felt much at all."

The jeep with them in it went down into the hollow where the huts had been built in the thin wood. Hales drove slowly, following the dim beam of the blackout headlights, until they saw the pale glimmer of the whitewashed stones outside the officers' mess.

It was when he was going up the path to the black-curtained doorway, with the glow of the lights inside against it and the sound of the voices coming out, that Mark began to miss David. He missed him all the time he was eating his supper with Hales, the dining-room dark and no cloth on the other tables because every one else had eaten before they got there. He kept missing him worse as the meal went on; not wanting to realize that he would not suddenly come through the door. And later on, when he was at the bar, he remembered that the first opportunity he got he would have to go and see David's father and mother.

The next morning it was raining and the clouds were swollen, dark and low across the sky. He had a shattering hangover and he could not remember a goddam thing about what he had done last night after a certain point. He was fully dressed except for one of his flying boots, and looking around for it he saw it put neatly in a corner. When he looked into it he saw he must have used it as a chamber pot at some stage, but he couldn't remember that either.

His hangover was so bad that he went along up the passage to Hales' room, limping slightly because he was still wearing only one flying boot. Hales was still asleep, looking relaxed and open and unworried, with the grey hair stuck out in spikes all over the middle of the pillow.

"Give me the keys to the jeep," said Mark, when he had wakened Hales up. "I want to go up to the flights."

"On the table," Hales said grunting and going back to sleep, drawing the sheet over his head.

Mark drove the jeep up to the runway and along it till he came to his plane. He got out and let the wind and rain blow on to him for a little; yawning and shivering with the stale sickness and the throbbing ache of the hangover.

He climbed into the plane and went crouching along the waist to his turret. He hooked up the short corrugated flex of his oxygen mask to a bottle of oxygen and clapped the mask to his nose, breathing deeply. After a while he felt much better. He kept feeling better all the way back to the hut. By the time he reached it the nausea was quite gone and he had only so much of a headache as to be almost a pleasant relief after what it had been like.

By midday, although they were all up at the flights, it was obvious there was going to be no flying. The weather had closed in hard, with a low cloud ceiling. And later on in the afternoon some of the crews were given twenty-four hours' leave. Mark was quite sure he wasn't going to remain on the station. He knew that missing somebody who was dead was a useless and exhausting occupation, particularly in the work they were doing. But, he decided, he was not going to stay here for the next twenty-four hours with nothing to do except remember yesterday afternoon and the empty room along the passage.

When he was dressing Hales came into the room. He sat on the edge of the bed in his rain-darkened, wet-smelling raincoat.

"You lucky aircrew," he said. "Always on leave, aren't you? Must be all that nerve-racking flying you do. Where are you going this time?"

"London," Mark told him. "I'll be able to get there about seven if you drive me down to the station."

"I would like to have just a part of all the unofficial petrol used in driving you people to stations," said Hales. "I wouldn't want all of it. Just a part. It would set me up for old age."

"The way you're going on," said Mark, "a man would think you had to buy it."

"All right," Hales said, "I'll drive you down. Don't get pox, though."

"If I do," said Mark, "you'll be the first to know. I promise you that."

On the way to the station Hales asked Mark, "Are you going to see David's people?"

"Of course," Mark told him. "But not this time. I don't think now would be a good time."

"No, I don't think so," said Hales. "Let them ride out the first bit of it together. I used to know a chap once. Feller called Duncan. Awfully nice chap, I knew him for years. His mother was almost a second mother to me. Looked on me as a sort of brother to this chap, you know; only I'd come along rather late in life. Anyway this chap got killed. It was during the last war. Bloody bad luck. Went outside for a pee and didn't come back because a heavy mortar blew him to hell. Bloody accident really, might just as well have been me. I wanted to pee too but was too lazy to get up. Both of us wanted to go badly but kept putting it off. Finally he went and that was that. Anyway I went to see his people the next time I was home on leave. They'd got over the first of it by then of course, but it was still pretty bad. You could see his mother asking herself why it had been him and not me. She hated herself for asking it, but you could see it there in her eyes. She couldn't help it really, we'd been so close, just like brothers."

"Thanks," said Mark. "I'll remember."

The train was almost full but he got a seat. It became more crowded further down the line but he didn't know it because right away as he had sat down he had fallen asleep; with his travel warrant stuck in his sleeve so the guard could take it without waking him up. He dreamt all the way of big writhing white flames roaring out of darkness, and himself standing on a platform looking at them and crying because he was frightened. When he woke up in London he felt his face to see if he had been really crying in his sleep.

Outside in the streets it was still raining and the ceiling of cloud had lowered. The light was pale and yellowish grey; everybody looked a little ill from the light. The city looked the way a city is in wartime: the buildings drab and stripped down and a little ugly. There were many uniforms everywhere and everybody was alert and held in, poised waiting for something to strike. It was more like a huge fort than a city. But you could feel the deep pulse and the old movements of the city underneath everything. It was something no fort would have had; something ancient and carefully grown. It was something much harder to destroy than the ragged gaps of bombed buildings. And you couldn't have destroyed it if you had killed half the people who still moved in the city. It went too deep and too far back for that: to destroy what he felt you would have had to raze everything and sow the ground with salt. That was one of the few ways you could kill a city. Bombs were only tactical manœuvres.

He went up, as he always did on these short leaves, to the club which put up officers from the Empire. Going into it was one of the few things nowadays that made him remember his race. And race, as it was there, was only something distinguishing you from a number of other people. Something that counted, but in the pleasantest way. Like your height or the shape of your face; an assertion of your uniqueness. Without noticing it he had come to accept, in this city and the club and among the men he met, the fact of this race.

It was a distinction but no difference: and though he realized it was dependent on the circumstances, he knew he would always have something of the way it was now.

At the club, Shirley Crewes was on duty at the desk. She was a big sallow girl with large clean features and heavy coils of dark hair. She had not seen her husband for the four years that he had been in prison camp and Mark knew that she had managed to keep faithful to him. She nearly hadn't more than once but she had won out so far. Mark always hoped she would because it would do something to her if she didn't.

The room was empty, so she hugged him, as she always did when he came in like this and there was no one around; holding him a little longer than was necessary. At first it had embarrassed him until he realized that she was not really holding on to him but to her husband.

"I want a room with a bath," he told her. "I really want a suite, but if you don't have one of those a room and bath will do."

She grinned at him.

"You can have a room with either a captain from Hong Kong or with a Wing Commander from New Zealand. And you can't have a bath because we're low in coal and we only have enough hot water for the wash basins. Which room do you want?"

"Give me the Chinese boy," he told her. "I hate to give up sharing a room with all that rank, but Occidentals snore."

She gave him the key and he went along to his room and shaved and shined his shoes.

Then he went out and ate a large meal of black-market duck in Soho and afterwards went into a pub and drank until ten o'clock.

When he came out the streets were dark and there were the muted beams of the blackout torches glimmering everywhere. He went along in the mesh of narrow streets between Leicester Square and Regent Street till he came to the corner where Moira had her beat.

Moira was a tall thin whore and he had gone with her one night when he was a little drunk. She had been quite marvellous in bed and she had grown very fond of him. Now every time he came to London he went with her for a night. She kept charging him less and less and the last time she had asked him to write her before he came up.

She was at her corner talking to a young American Airforce major and Mark passed them so close she could make him out. Then he walked on and waited in the darkness for a couple of minutes and walked back again. She was alone.

"Hullo," he said. "How did you get rid of him?"

"I told him it was ten pounds for a short time," she said, smiling. "For a moment there I thought he was going to take it. Those boys have so much money. Why didn't you write me?"

"I only came up an hour or two ago; I'm going back tomorrow."

"Oh," she said, in a disappointed way. "You want to come home with me?"

"Of course."

At her place, in the powder-scented, other-men-smelling, oversoft bed, she was eager, intricate and giving. It was pretty good and not like the furtive uneasiness of most of the other whores he had been with.

Afterwards she began to cry beside him and would not tell him why she was crying. She insisted on going to sleep with her arms around him and he found it very uncomfortable at first, but after a while he went to sleep too.

In the morning she took the money he had given her the night before and held it out to him silently; standing there in an ugly pink nightdress with her thin pointed breasts and long, thin legs showing through. He did not want to take it at first; but then he saw it was to her a matter of great importance and he took the notes and put them back into his wallet. She became very gay after that and cooked an enormous breakfast which he had difficulty in eating. All through breakfast she kept making extremely funny, spontaneous jokes at which he found himself laughing very easily.

Going back to camp on the train the weather began to clear. By the time he was walking along the short cut through the fields the sun had begun to show through a watery film of cloud.

When he got back to the station, he went over to

Headquarters, and then across to the mess to look for his mail. There were no letters and he went into the lounge. The big cream and blue room was almost empty except for two Australian officers in their dark blue uniforms, who were reading, and for Buxton, his captain, who was playing chess with Tiny Mansfield, their navigator, at one of the card tables.

He went up to them. Buxton had hunched his long, grotesquely thin body into the peculiar knot which was his position of relaxation. Tiny Mansfield was pink and restless, fidgeting, and making small distressed noises between his teeth. This usually occurred when he played against Buxton.

"Hullo, Mark," said Buxton, raising his gnarled, untidy face with its long slitted eyes, "had a good leave?"

"Fair," said Mark. "You?"

"Good enough. Briefing at oh four hundred."

"I know," said Mark. "They told me over at H.Q." He looked at the board.

Buxton had opened with a slashing, risky knight and bishop attack, his pawns well up. Tiny as usual had been too timid in opening, keeping everything well back and entrenched. He had not lost many yet, but very shortly his pieces would begin to get in each other's way.

"I keep telling him," Mark said to Buxton, "that he'll never play chess like that. You'll have him in about ten moves, Bux."

Tiny looked up indignantly. "Please . . . keep . . .

out . . . of . . . this," he said through his clenched teeth. "I know what I'm doing."

He moved a pawn, but kept his hand on it, moved it back, thought aloud in agonized whispers, then moved another pawn one square.

Mark shook his head, clicking his tongue sorrowfully.

"Go away," Tiny said furiously. "Go far away. I was doing all right till you came."

Mark grinned at the gravely smiling Buxton and went out of the lounge, out of the mess, and along the path to his billet.

At the door of the billet he paused and looked down the long, dim corridor and at the synonymous, green painted doors. He was suddenly empty and lonely with a great longing to see David again. He had a wishful conviction that if he called his name loudly enough he would be able to see him walking along the shadowy corridor. That he might even reply. Almost helplessly he said loudly, "David." Then he stood there for a moment, feeling very foolish.

He went to his room and put down his bag and stood looking out of the window. The sky was beginning to thicken again. Fat, smudged rain-clouds massing in the east. He hoped, longingly, that it would close in badly and prevent flying tomorrow. The thought of flying again so quickly made him feel tired and faintly sick with indefinite fear. After a while he went to his bed and lay there, thinking of Moira and David's fair, gentle, good-looking face.

81

He woke up with the sound of his door closing and, opening his eyes, saw Hales standing by his bed. He looked gratefully up at the big scarred face. He was glad that Hales had come in to see him, now.

"Hullo," he said.

"Good leave?" asked Hales. "I looked for you in the mess, but I might have known when you boys aren't on leave you're sleeping."

Mark grinned. "It's tough it wasn't like this in your war," he said, "but we've made progress since then."

He got up and went to the little dressing-table for his cigarettes. Then he turned, and, standing by the dresser, he told Hales about Moira and, after that, of how he had called to David in the hope that he might answer. Hales nodded.

"I can understand that," he said. "Don't feel foolish because you did it. Everybody tries something when they're missing someone very much. At first, anyway. Afterwards they don't bother to try."

"How do I act when I see his parents?" Mark asked him. "What do I say?"

Hales shook his head. "I don't know," he replied. "I really don't know, Mark. Say something . . . you'll have to. But we don't have any words to cover the situation of death. Priests say they do, but then the dead have never been able to tell us if the priests are right."

He stopped and looked hard at Mark for a moment. "I tried to write David's mother last night. Unofficially. To say how sorry I was and what he'd been like for his friends; you know the sort of thing. I didn't finish it, though."

"Why?" Mark asked him.

"I wasn't saying the right things. The boy I was writing about wasn't David Lumsden. He was somebody from the time when I was that age. You see what I'm getting at?"

"Not quite," said Mark, "but go on. I'd like to understand, Tommy."

"What I mean," Hales gestured gropingly with his big hand, "is what sort of men are you and David and Buxton and a few of the others. The best of you, I mean. The rest are much the same in any age: a gut, a small vocabulary, a few children to follow on. But I haven't been able to understand the people like you and David. Not as much as I've wanted."

"That always happens, doesn't it?" said Mark. "It's hard for one generation to understand the one after it. Maybe that's why children get on better with their grandparents than with anyone else."

"No Mark," Hales shook his head. He got up and went to the window with his long, deliberate stride and looked out. "Doesn't look like flying tomorrow," he muttered. "It's not just age, Mark. It's been a shift in values. I don't mean simply in art or sex; it's something else. Sometimes I listen to you boys talking in the mess. Even when you disagree with each other, you still seem to be talking a sort of shorthand which you all recognize. It makes me feel almost excluded."

"Not you, Tommy," Mark told him. "I wouldn't want you excluded at any time."

"I know," said Hales, "and yet you take things for granted that I can understand only when I think about them."

"Like what?" Mark urged him.

Hales frowned. "Not just generalities," he said, "but specific things. Like . . . patriotism for instance. No, let me finish. You're still ready to fight and be killed in the name of a country. But England, say, doesn't mean what it meant just before our war, or even during it, when we began to get sickened. With you people the country isn't the thing; it's the concept or an idea; something that states a way of life."

"But Tommy," Mark said. "That's how the war developed. That's just the way things were."

"I know that, too," Hales replied. "For some reason the focus of the world really and finally changed in that respect; and it made people to fit into that focus. It became a matter of persuasions, and your country was only a piece of the pattern. I was only trying to say that your age accepts this without any effort at all. I have to remember to accept it."

"That may be true," Mark said slowly. "I hadn't thought about it, but I guess you're right. Do you think it's such an important difference?"

"Yes," Hales said, smiling. He was more relaxed now that he had begun to order his thought. "Not for itself, perhaps, but it comes out of something that's very important. The big thing."

"What?"

"Private happiness," Hales waited, as if expecting Mark to say something, then he continued. "It's not easy to explain, but your generation doesn't seem to have any real regard for private happiness. Your own or anyone else's."

"I don't know," Mark said. "Every man wants to be happy. Look at the way we go after it on leave; listen to any popular song. I don't quite get what you're driving at."

Hales laughed. "I don't think you do," he said. "In a way it embarrasses you for me to mention it. I don't mean you don't like being happy. I only meant that private ambitions, in the way of love for instance, are never pure and unattached with you. Love, for your generation, is only interesting and important if it takes place inside a much wider frame than two people together can make. The same with anything else; every private thing has a responsibility to something bigger that seems to enter every corner of your lives. Even when you're not aware of it, as *you* aren't, Mark, it lies on your conscience. Whether you admit or not, you secretly distrust the time you have to spend on being individuals; you think it's dangerous."

"I don't agree with you," Mark said. "At least I don't agree with everything. I don't think we have as much time for the things that you had, but we like being ourselves just as much."

Hales moved to the door and opened it. He looked at Mark, who was slowly buttoning his tunic and straightening his tie before the looking-glass. Mark's forehead was faintly creased and he was scarcely glancing at himself in the mirror.

Hales smiled wryly and fondly at his back.

"You know, Mark," he said, "I'm glad I'm not your age. Your world seems to ask all the right questions about people and give all the wrong answers about individuals."

"It's the only world we've got," Mark said, joining him at the door. "Come on, let's go and get a sherry before dinner."

Outside, they both stopped to look at the sky. It was thick, grey and low and a small gusty breeze was beginning to stir the grass before the billet. With a sense of great relief, Mark realized that it would probably be too bad for the planes to go up in the morning. . . .

PART THREE: ECHOES

1

Now that the people had gone out of the lane everything that happened in the room seemed too intimate. You could hear the voices and see faces so clearly that it embarrassed you a little.

A man passed under the window. He was drunk and he was singing something he had made up himself:

> "We kill de white man dem to-day,
> We kill de brown man dem to-day,
> Kill de white man,
> Kill de brown man;
> What a kill we kill to-day."

They heard the soft baritone, quiet and mad, fade out of the top end of the lane.

There were a few of the women and some children who passed, talking of the riot. But, except for these, everything had left them.

"The people will stick to main roads," Mark told them. "They always do. If they get into the suburbs, into St. Andrew, they'll go down the side streets. But down here they'll go along the main drags, like blood along an artery."

"I still think I could make it out there."

"No," Mark said. "I don't want you to try. You might make it, but a thousand to one you wouldn't. You'd have to cross Queen Victoria Street and go past the market, and sure as God they'd jump you before that. Let them come to us."

He spoke finally and he knew Ted would listen to what he said. He wondered if the woman had got through to the police station and if once she got there they would think him important enough to send a patrol down for him. He knew they would. If they had any men they would. He had known the time that he had become important in the politics of his country. Although he was not in the House and he hoped he never would be, he was still much too important for them to let him die. He had made too many speeches. Too many bloody, empty speeches. Jesus Christ, but any man who could make nothing sound so good as he had done deserved to be rescued. Yes, by God, he was a great boy all right. The answer to everything right there. Salvation and redemption all here on the platform, ladies and gentlemen, my people, my new country, my race of the future. Rest your hopes and your passions, your sins and your sorrows right here with the People's Party and Mark Lattimer its prophet. Give unto me your brains and your bellies and we shall fill them and all manner of things shall be well. Don't tell them, of course, that you've had a full belly all your life without it helping you much. You are different, you are the boy with the words; you've got a great, beautiful, bourgeois soul; you've got problems. These are only the people. Not a number of distinct, suffering souls, but the people. The only things they should worry about you can fix. You're a great fixer, all right. Look how you fixed everybody you ever touched; fixed them good. And now you dear trusting people you, you tender grass on which I feed, step up and Mark Lattimer will dish out the manure. Hot and sweet from the party stables.

"To hell with the party," said Mark Lattimer, without bitterness.

"Sure," said Ted. "I've often thought that was a good place for it. But we can't send it there yet. Not now or here. There's a time for everything."

"To hell with you too," said Mark. "In fact, to hell with the whole goddam world."

When he heard Brysie gulp back her tears he made himself stop. He used everything he had left from all he had spent and made himself stop. Whatever happened now he could not make Brysie cry. Not because he was going on so and afraid to die. Somewhere or other a man had to put up a decent show. The good ones did it most of the time for all their lives so that you wondered what it was they were drawing on to do it. You wondered where they got the faithfulness. The other ones, like himself, tried to do it now when it was too late. When it couldn't do any good. And they didn't make a very convincing job of trying. Not like his father had done. Good to the end because he had been good all the way through. . . .

. . . His father had loved the mountains of the island and when Mark was growing up they used to go for long trips in the green forests, right up among the mists and the clouds.

But that had been a long time ago, and the year his father was dying slowly they were not in a place you could see the mountains as they had been able to do in the old home under the foothills.

That year his father died was the year Mark had come home. He did not make much money that year, and with his father sick as he had been for a long time there was not much left from the business.

So they moved down from the foothills; to a place in the plains where all you could see was the drab stems and the bronze-green fronds of coconut palms and the tough dry trees of the savannah. They were not poor, but it was not much of a place for a man to die in. At nights the moon was big and hot and the smell of dust and the stale, slightly rancid odour of the savannah hung in the air. The dogs howled all night, and there were some Chinese next door who were good neighbours but played what seemed like one Oriental record all day.

What he remembered about his father was how he had lain all day sweating in the bed because he was too weak to move. They used to keep all the doors and windows open but in the bedroom it was still pretty hot. The old man had lain there and sweated all through that extraordinary, hot, dry season. And when the cancer in his rectum had eaten far up into him he sweated as much from the constant pain as from the heat. Two or three times a day they used to change the sheets.

Mark could always tell when the slow, gut-drawing-out pain was on the old man. His eyes in the skull face would glow brightly and for a moment they would shade with the possibility of surrender. Then he would breathe deeply and smile at Mark and ask him how the West Indians had done against the English in the cricket. He got very indignant the time the English gave the West Indies a bad pitch to bat on at Old Trafford. "They would never have dared try that with Don Bradman," he had said. "The Australians would have refused to play on a disgraceful wicket like that. And very rightly too."

He would ask Mark lots of other things too. Nearly everything of importance that was occurring outside Mark would be expected to know. The old man did not question him greedily either, or fearfully, trying to suck energy from the healthy world. Everything Mark told him was considered and discussed with great objectivity. Also he used to laugh and joke so that sometimes you forgot how yellow and skeletal he looked in the dank sheets and laughed with him.

Right there at the end everything had seemed to pile up on the old man. So much indignity and agony that was unable to break him.

He wasn't weighing more than eighty or ninety pounds then: the body was so thin that the skull head looked huge and grotesque. The skin was a dull, greasy yellow with the unexcreted overflow of waste into the blood. He stank worse than anything you had ever imagined; coming into the room you could feel your throat catch involuntarily on the smell. And even on the verandah outside you had it blown to you sometimes on a stray eddy of air. He could not go to the toilet like other people but had to have a tube in his side and it took about two hours to empty his bowels; and sometimes it would begin to come out before he could signal for the pan. He had to be washed and changed like a baby, then, because he was too weak to lift a teaspoon of wine to his mouth.

All this had been unable to break the old man. Once it nearly broke him. That was the night he had told Mark and Mark's mother to go out of the room and when they came back they saw that he had been crying but that it was all finished with now and whatever he had fought was down and would never be able to come back.

About two weeks before he died he used to tell Mark a lot about himself. How it used to be growing up on a property in the old days. And how he got lost in the John Crow mountains one time and walked for three days without water, and how they found the river that would lead them down to the coast only to get nearly drowned when the cloud-burst in the high mountains filled the river with foaming water. All this time he was not really a man. He was an envelope filled with unbelievable agony who writhed slowly and dreadfully at intervals between stained sheets. But the part of him that was left as a man became bigger before Mark's eyes every time he came into the room; until it was something so completely fine that he almost failed to understand it.

Then one night Mark heard him give two enormous shuddering breaths and he thought it was all over. But it wasn't and the old man lived on till morning, when he could not speak but only smiled at Mark with great sweetness and winked slowly and Mark had left then to go to work. And when he had come back, after the telephone call that said his father was dead, his mother had told him the last words the old man had been able to utter.

"Tell Mark," his father had said, "that he is the best son I could have wished for. Tell him I love him. Be sure to tell him that."

His mother said that was exactly how his father had spoken. She said he had spoken with great emphasis and precision.

That was the year he didn't have enough money to take a house where his father could see the mountains. And it was the year his father was too weak to go driving, so he never saw the mountains at all. . . .

2

"I'm sorry," he told Brysie and Ted, "for that little business a minute ago."

"Don't be silly, boy," Ted said. "This hanging around is getting on my nerves too."

"Darling," said Brysie, "please don't talk too much. Just rest, eh? Just rest and try and sleep." She began to pass her hand lightly and lovingly over his forehead and softly through the coarse, damp brown curls of his hair. She leaned over him and smiled and kissed her fingertips and put them gently on his eyelids.

Mark moved his head slightly and with an impatience he tried to hide. He was weak; weaker than he had ever felt, and the pain in his side was like being struck methodically with a heavy metal bar. But he did not want to be quiet and he knew that he would not sleep. His death was back in the room; stinking and oppressive; and he had begun to be afraid of it again.

"I was thinking of my old man," he told them. "He was a hell of a good man to know. I wish he were here now. God, but he was a good chap to have around."

Nobody said anything because there is little comment you can make when a man is talking about his father, then Brysie said: "I remember your old man, Mark. I met him once. Not socially, but I remember meeting him."

"Oh, yes! You never told me. When did you meet him?"

"Oh, it's just something I remembered. When I was a little girl. I had bad eyes and my father brought me up to town to have them seen to. We had a good crop that year and he could afford it. I don't know who told him about your dad, but that's the one we went to. I thought the instruments in your father's office were going to hurt and I started to cry. My father got embarrassed and said: "Excuse her, sah, she is a naughty chile. Chile, stop your bawling." He said that quite fiercely because he was embarrassed. But your father just took me and told me what all the instruments were for and let me work the charts on the wall. I remember he fixed something with mirrors so I could look back into my own eye and see all the red veins against the white. Then he said I didn't need glasses, but that I should do some eye exercises that he would show me how to do. And he did, right there in the office, rolling his eyes about. I was fascinated. My father was a little disappointed, I think, at not being able to get glasses for me from a posh oculist. But I did those exercises. I did them till it's a wonder my eyes didn't drop out of my head. I think I must have felt that if I did them like I promised, your father would marry me, or maybe adopt me. And I didn't just remember this. I've remembered it all along, but this is the first time it has come up naturally."

"That's the old man," said Mark, feeling a warm,

sad and wonderful glow go through him. He chuckled gently and pressed on Brysie's hand.

"So that's why you love me? Just a Freudian throw-back. Just marrying my old man."

"Fool," she said, and kissed his cheek.

"Give me a little water," he said. "My mouth is dry. Just a little to wet my mouth."

Ted brought the mug and Brysie raised his head and held it for him to drink. He lay back again.

Yes, he told himself, talking was much better. So long as you had enough left that talking wasn't an intolerable effort, it was much better if they allowed you conversation. It did not make you forget anything you had done, or how you felt, but it made them much easier.

"How do you feel?" asked Ted. He was always asking that. The silence must make him uncomfortable too, thought Mark.

"O.K." he said, not meaning to lie. He never wanted to lie to these people, and when he said he felt all right he was not really lying. He felt his strength going, but slowly, almost leisurely. It was not a quick, appalling drain as it had been that other time when he was wounded. I'm on a slow ebb, he thought, and maybe if they get to me in time they'll save my skin. I don't think so, but they just might, so I can say I'm O.K.

Aloud he said: "He got me in the subscapular. It runs under the arm, near the armpit. And I think he must have done some damage inside. I'll be O.K. when the doctors get at me, but it's a hell of a wound for amateurs to deal with."

"What's keeping them?" asked Brysie. "Jesus Christ, what's keeping them? That woman should have been there by now."

"Don't you know there's a riot on?" Mark joked her. Then he asked Ted, "What's the time?"

"About half past eleven," said Ted.

"Do you know," said Mark, "that we've only been here about an hour and a half? God, it seems like a month."

Outside, in the lane, it was dead still. Still in the white dancing heat and the dryness. The heat and the light were white now against the window; and the quiet of the lane was lonely and strange. But if you listened long enough in silence you could hear the murmur of the tension in all the homes around them, where the children and some of the women still were. And every now and again a muffled, sinister explosion of violence reached the room from what was taking place up in the city.

His left leg had gone to sleep now. He could feel the familiar, not there numbness that was like being frozen without the cold. It went like that from time to time, ever since it had healed from the mess the Luftwaffe bullet had made. It did not discommode him in any other way except this, that it sometimes went to sleep when he had been in one position too long.

"Will you rub my leg?" he asked Brysie. "It's going to sleep on me."

She smiled and turned back the cover. She undid his trousers and put her hand down the loosened top and he could feel her thin, gentle, very strong fingers, kneading the flesh and muscle around the jagged ridge of scar tissue on his thigh. She had a good hand and it was not long before he felt the tingle in his foot and the sensation of being alive return to his leg.

"That's it," he told her. "That's fine. It feels all right now."

She smiled and ran her hand very gently up his left side and rested it protectively on his heart. Then she covered him again.

It was a damn lucky break, he thought, it was just damn luck. I was bloody careless that day, and if I'd got more than this for it I couldn't have a thing to say about it. You can forgive a lot of things to yourself, and make them up. But you mustn't ever try to forgive yourself the times you're careless. The times you fail to do what you know about. All the same it's the most personal and the only private things I have. This scar on my thigh and the one low down on my belly. I've never told anyone about those really. Perhaps because I wouldn't know how to start. When they have asked I've told them how it looked. The mechanics. But not the way it was; the way it felt. . . .

. . . He could see the sky as it had been coming back that day after they had been hit.

It had been an autumn day, hard and bright as

steel; very blue, with the pale ribs of alto-cirrus ice across the deep sky.

They had been hit as they turned out of the bombing run, in that vulnerable moment between the turn and the climb. And they had not known until halfway back whether they would make it or not.

The enemy fighter that attacked them had been flown by a very good pilot. He had brought it in out of the sun and Mark had felt the drumming shake of the fighter's bullets in the fuselage before he saw it as it went past and down, dropping under the bomber.

He had said calmly, "Me. 109, going away, five o'clock down, about three hundred," and his stomach was empty and greasy as he swung his turret and tried to lead the going away fighter, firing and seeing his tracers shine in the empty sky.

The fighter had gone out and away, banking over, so that the angle of fire between the rear turret and the mid-upper was cut unfavourably. It had gone far out till Mark had lost it but knew it was out there turning up and back like a shark flicking over in the deep blue water.

He had swung his turret slowly, trying to see everything in the hard, bright sky behind the bomber. And he had picked it up as it began the fast, deadly curve of pursuit, slipping one wing down the sky, not seeming to go forward much but swelling larger and nearer with enormous quickness.

All the time he kept telling the rest of the crew what he saw. Trying to say it with great exactness, keeping his voice steady and unemotional, trying to give the rest of them the precise picture of what the enemy fighter was doing.

Then he had closed his hands round the triggers and could hear the roaring of his guns and the rattling clank as the cartridge belts fed into the four, furiously clutching breeches. He had known that everything depended on how well he shot because the bomber was damaged and could not do much evasive action.

He had fired in long, shortly spaced bursts until he did not have to lead the fighter with the red circle of his reflector sight, but had it right inside.

It had been huge then, stubby and menacing, and at that point it had seemed to be coming right into the turret with an implacable, devouring rush. He had seen his tracers all around it and there had been the one panic, unbelieving second when he knew he was not going to hit it.

The enemy pilot had held his fire till just before the breakaway. And Mark had seen it coming in unhit, and then the stuttering, explosive blossoms of orange flame as it fired dead on.

There had been a rapid thudding somewhere above his head and almost immediately the incredible smashing blows in his left leg and low down in his side, and after that the pain, deep-hurting and with a horrible surge of cold, sweating nausea. And he had bent over his gun sight putting his hand weakly to his side trying to grab the hurt as the grey, deep mists came over his eyes.

Echoes

He had not known when the fighter broke off the attack; for what reason no one could understand, unless it was that it had been on a strike and only had enough ammunition left for two passes at the bomber.

Going back the rest of the way Mark had been quite sure he was going to die. They had laid him out in the waist, and the pain was still there and the sickness, but the worst thing had been the terror.

Oh please, he had said to himself, oh please don't make me die. Oh God, I don't want to die, oh please God, I don't want to die. He had kept saying that the whole way back, quite sure he was going to die, and terrified.

Then the next thing he knew they had come down in France and it was hot and bright outside the plane. A man was bending over him; he had on a white coat and he looked huge. And Mark was grinning at him because he was hardly hurting any more and the fact that he was going to live was of great importance. . . .

3

I wonder, he asked himself, what the hell it is happening inside me? I am hurting like blazes outside, but I expected that. But it's inside I can't make out. I feel as if I'm a column of sand and the sea was swirling away at my perimeter and every minute a little bit of the column dissolves. It must be the blood pressure. Oh God, I wish I could stop leaking blood.

I wish I could stop being afraid. I wish I was out of here. I wish the old man was here. He'd know what to do. Not that these two aren't the best people I've known. You hear that, death; old comrade, old bastard; don't crowd me, death, let me enjoy these people a little longer.

He had a moment of hard and furious anger at death that filled his mouth with bitter-tasting emptiness. And it passed, leaving only the heavy fear that he couldn't get rid of.

He looked up at Brysie, trying to see her so plainly he would never forget a single thing about her face.

"Say something," he asked.

"What?" she smiled, running her finger down the side of his cheek.

"Oh, I don't know. Anything. Anything at all."

"All right then, where shall I take you for your holiday?"

"What holiday?"

"The holiday you're going to need when this is over, when you're better."

O.K., Mark said silently, I might as well play along. I'll play along right up to where I'm too tired to play any more: because Brysie is the best people I've ever known and you can't ever try too much for the people who've been kind to you. Also I can forget that leering bastard at the foot of the bed who's coming for me pretty soon; if I play along a bit I can forget him.

"I don't need a holiday," he said, joking her along.

"As soon as this foolishness is over there'll be plenty work to do."

"Now, darling, don't be silly. Of course you need a rest; you haven't had one since before I knew you. You're as stale as window bread. Three years ago they'd never have chopped you, you'd have seen them coming."

"I guess I'm just an old punch drunk fighter," said Mark. "Anyway, I don't know where to go for a holiday."

"Of course you do," she said crisply and maternally. "There's the hills. We can go up there. I don't mean like when you and Ted go into the bush after wild hog. I mean the nice comfortable hills where you can drive up to the front door. You can borrow Lewis's cottage."

That's the voice they all get, thought Mark. No matter how they look or where they come from or what their education has been. All of them, the good ones, they talk just like that when they mean you to do something for your own good. A real woman is the most amazing thing you're likely to meet in this life. You kick like hell when you're not sick and you have to take them along with you. But if you don't have them, anything you do doesn't mean a goddam thing. If you don't have a voice like that somewhere around you might as well be dead.

"Ted," he said.

"Yes, boy?" Ted replied.

"Don't ever forget," Mark told him, "to be

astonished when somebody is kind to you and somebody loves you. Always expect it and always be
astonished at it."

"Right you are, boy," Ted said. "I'll make a note
of it. You're sure of it?"

"Absolutely," said Mark smiling.

He looked at Ted; at the smiling, almost gaunt, very
young face, and the dark eyes serious with new
thought behind the smile. He saw him with a disturbing clarity that felt almost presumptuous; as if he were
seeing too much. He'll be a hell of a good older man,
he thought. He'll be something damn fine and I wish
I could be there to see it.

"What happens," asked Ted; his voice was light
and yet oddly searching, as it was, always, when he
wanted to know. "What happens, exactly, to you or
what you're doing when you forget to be . . . 'astonished' . . . by kindness and love?"

"It's hard to say exactly," Mark said. "Perhaps
we don't value them enough. But everything bad
seems to start when you forget to be astonished by
them. That's why politics is such a sad thing. It's sad
any way you play it. Sadder than war even. Because
you get tied up in the procedure and think up reasons
why you should have kindness and love. You acquire
a set of rules about those things and you try to act on
the rules first and feel afterwards. It works in a way
because it's the only way we know how to do it. But
it doesn't work very well and it takes the guts out
of you."

He knew he was getting serious and maybe he was preaching. But he wanted to bring out this thing that was one of the things he had learnt. He wanted, if it were possible, to leave something more of himself for these two than the stink of his fear and his death.

"Politics aren't like that with you," said Ted. He said it with one of those rare lapses of his into complete seriousness and positive judgement that always surprised you because it was so pure and without arrogance. "Politics aren't like that with you at all. If they were I would have left you long ago. I wouldn't have stuck around."

He looked very old sitting there, leaning forward, with his chin on his fist and the broad spare-fleshed Indian face quite grave.

"I was getting like it," Mark said. "The slogans were taking me over. The way they've taken over Frankie Malloy and Tubby Lopez. You know—'The People's Friend', 'A Man of the People'. That sort of thing. You get to believe after a while. You see yourself in capital letters, and them too. It's safer that way. After a while they aren't souls any more. They're the New Jamaica or some crap like that."

You couldn't help it, he thought. You got careless or lazy or both and it happened to you. You talked so much about suffering and poverty, that you became abstract. You got economics like a disease. And you forgot how to feel about suffering and poverty. Or about anything else for that matter. Unless you were lucky and had people like Brysie and the old man and

Ted to remind you. To remind you how much faithfulness you had lost. . . .

. . . Now he was in London that time his wife had left him and he was living with Maginot, the Trinidadian student, in the flat above the canal. It had been a street full of colonials and Jews and refugees from a dozen countries. A street of exiles, and you could always feel how different it was and how much nearer to sadness than any other street you knew. Some of the people in the street, the West Indians and the girls from Europe especially, used to wear very bright colours. But the clothes never looked very gay; they always looked as if they were trying to merge into the dun of the buildings, trying to achieve a protective camouflage for the aliens who wore them.

That was the time he and Maginot knew a ship's steward who smuggled them in half a dozen bottles of rum from the Jamaica run, and they gave a party.

The English students who came to the party were quite unaccustomed to the sort of liquor Maginot and he had provided. As the level went down in the bottles they all became a little foolish.

The fat, ugly girl who was a communist, and who had once been very zealous in the Catholic Church, spread her arms against the walls in a crucifix. She shouted, "I want to die for the people: Oh God, let me die for the wonderful, wonderful people." She shouted this several times with the English students trying to make her keep quiet. Then she passed out and had to be put to bed in Mark's room. He had spread newspapers all round the bed, and on it, for when she was going to be sick.

The English students had been very embarrassed, but Maginot had been very impressed.

It was, he told Mark afterwards, a real slice of life. . . .

4

"You've got to do it alone," he said.

"Do what, dear?" asked Brysie.

"Anything that means a damn thing."

"Yes, dear."

"You try and share it," he went on, "but you can't. In the end you have to do it alone."

"Please don't talk too much, Mark darling. Just rest."

"It would make a beautiful tragedy," Mark said. "Wouldn't it, Ted?"

"I don't know, boy," Ted replied. "I hadn't thought about it."

"Or a beautiful comedy," said Mark. "A beautiful something anyway. But it would need a good man to tell it."

Stop that now, he told himself. Don't do anything to spoil this for them. Don't muck this one up. But it's true all the same. You try and share it and in the end you have to do it alone. . . .

· · ·

. . . That spring in California he and David had come up from the coast, hitchhiking through the mountains because they had spent all their money with two splendid, hospitable girls in Los Angeles.

It had been pretty good hitchhiking. You had been able to take your choice of lifts: when they saw the uniform they used to stop and offer to pick you up. The mountains had been yellow and green with spring and the air had been a clear, positive pleasure to breathe.

They had stopped at that roadside café and hung around joking and chatting with the girl who ran it, waiting for a truck to come so they could get a long lift. The child had come in then and said, "Mamma, there is a funny mans sleeping in the field." They had smiled at her and gone on talking. And she had come in later, saying, "The funny mans is still sleeping. Mamma, he looks so funny," and he and David had gone into the long, dusty-smelling grass of the field and found the old Negro man lying sick under a mimosa bush. They had carried him back to the café, their shoulders under his arms, his feet dragging whish-whish through the grass. He had felt no heavier than a half-empty kit-bag and had been shivering with fever.

In the café, after they had given him some coffee and bread out in the kitchen, he had told them he was going down to Texas to see his daughter who was sick. He had sat there, telling them, blinking his red, ill eyes, and with a grey scum at the corner of his lips.

"You're sick," Mark had told him. "You'd better go into hospital."

"No, suh," the old Negro man had said. "I can't stop now. My daughter is sick. Bad sick. She's goin' to need her folks, and I'm the only folks she has."

In a while he had gone out into the sun and set off down the road, walking slowly and shaking with the fever.

Mark and David had given him three of the big, solid-feeling silver dollars you get in the West and the old man had taken the money and put it in a frayed empty purse.

He would not be doing this, he had told them, but for his daughter being sick. She was all alone in Houston, he said, and she had been a good daughter to him. . . .

PART FOUR: THE DEATH

"You hear it now?" Mark asked them. He had lifted his head off the pillow and they could see him frowning intently.

"What?" asked Ted. "I don't hear anything."

"Listen," he told them, then they heard it.

The sound of the rifles came rattling clearly through the muted, undisciplined stir of the riot up town. At first it seemed as if the sound of the rioting was gone, leaving only the echo of the rifles. Then they heard the rifles again and the harsh drift of the massed voices up town was still there.

"They've begun to close in," Mark told them. "They must be moving the police and the soldiers down the main roads from the suburbs. But the boys in the city won't know it yet. What you heard was the mopping up further out."

He could see Ted at the end of the bed looking sick. And when he turned his eyes up to Brysie's face it was harsh and taut and she held herself as if she were trying to listen with her whole body. He had known

The Death

from the time the riot started that it would end like
this. All the time lying here he had known it and
waited for it. But knowing it didn't make it any easier
to listen to now.

"Look," he said softly. "It won't be as bad as it
sounds, you know. They'll fire the first couple of
rounds high. If that breaks the people then they'll
just let them go."

"Suppose it doesn't break the crowds," asked Ted,
slowly and flatly. "What happens then?"

"It all depends," Mark told him. "It all depends
on how they look. If they just stand there and try and
work themselves up the police and the soldiers will
probably fire another round. Not so high this time.
Low enough for them to really hear the bullets. Then
they'll fix bayonets and advance. And that ought to
scatter the crowd. It all depends, too, on the officers.
If they're good and handle the thing scientifically
nobody ought to get hurt. But you have to be very
cool and detached in a riot. You have to keep remembering that you're not there to kill anybody. It's
not easy to remember when you're not sure whether
a crowd will charge or not."

And if the crowd does charge, he thought then, if
they break and try to swamp the rifles and the
bayonets, that's your fault if you're the officer who's
trying to break up a section of the riot. It's all your
fault because if you're a good officer you can destroy
the confidence of a mob without hurting any of them
in it. But it takes a hell of a good man to make all the

111

right decisions at the right moments. It is the saddest and filthiest and most difficult sort of fighting there is. All fighting is sad and filthy and difficult. But this business in the streets, where one side is your own people and not armed and not led scientifically, is worse than anything war can show. Every time somebody gets killed in this you have failed in your business. This riot hasn't done me any good, but I'm glad I'm not an officer trying to break it up. Trying to disintegrate the mobs and send the people off down the side streets, frightened but not hurt. You have to be really good stuff to split the focus of a mob without bloodshed. Maybe you have to be so good that they shouldn't give the job to policemen or soldiers but to people much wiser.

They heard the rolling crackle of rifle fire again. It was distant and muted but it had the hard, sinister crispness gunfire has no matter how far or how near it is to you. There was the constant murmuring clamour of riot in the city; and very faintly out of the dying sound of rifles a new human note, urgent, splintered and with an unmistakable signature of panic.

"Mark," said Ted, "what happens if the crowd doesn't break? If the people don't go home like good little boys, what happens then?"

"Easy, Ted," Mark told him. "Take it easy, boy. That won't do you any good. Brysie darling, don't tense up like that. Relax, both of you, until you have something to do. You're in the middle of a fight that

112

started long before any of us was born and will be going on long after we're dead. And any time you're in a fight you ought to save all your strength when you're not actually fighting. Don't waste it in worrying about things you can't help."

Oh God, he thought, listen to me. I must sound like an owl. Still that's a privilege I've earned being nearly dead and all. I'm a condemned man, aren't I, so I'll just have that hearty breakfast of moralizing. I'll preach the bloody ears off them. Oh dammit to hell, damn this pain and damn, double damn, this blasted weakness. God, but it's hot in here; this room is cooking me like an oven.

The walls of the room, the gaudy picture on the wall at the foot of the bed, Ted's face and the sounds from outside began to dissolve around him. They blurred and ran liquidly together in the hot, white-shot, colour-shot, going to grey of his pain and weakness. He lay clutching Brysie's hand, dimly aware that he was holding it; feeling the bed lift and sway under him. Then it passed and his mind was clear again: he did not think it had lasted more than a second. He was more afraid, now, than at any time since he had been chopped.

But I ought to do something for Ted and Brysie, he told himself. I ought to try and say something that will make this easier for them. They both feel what is happening outside more than I. I know it better, but it doesn't hurt me as much. The people out there aren't part of me. They're part of Ted though. Not

completely, yet, but they will be some day. He's
given his allegiance from the heart. I gave it from the
head. And that's why I was afraid this morning; I
didn't have any heart to fall back on. They knew it,
the people out there; the people I've tried to love.
They smelt out the failure, and the fear; that's why
they chopped me.

"Ted," he said.

"Yes?"

"If the crowd charges when the police and the
soldiers tell them to go, it needn't be as bad as you
think, you know."

"No?" said Ted.

"No. The troops will get orders to fire at their legs
first. That may stop them. If it doesn't then they'll
use the tear-gas. It will be ugly as hell, but they'll try
not to kill."

"If I didn't feel so helpless," said Brysie. She got
and went with jerky swiftness to the window. They
could see her gripping the sill, hard. "We're just stuck
here and Mark is hurt and all that is happening out
there. And we can't do a damn thing. Jesus."

"Brysie," said Mark. "Please, Brysie darling, don't
go on like that."

"Oh, Mark, I'm sorry." She ran back from the
window and knelt quickly beside the bed. She took
one of his hands very gently between both of hers.
"I'm sorry, Mark, I didn't mean to go on like that.
Darling! Your hand is as cold as ice."

There was so much alarm in her voice that Ted got

up quickly. He came up beside her and stood looking down at Mark. His face was mask-stiff with worry and he was biting his lower lip.

"It's all right, really," Mark told them. He could hear how weak his voice sounded.

"Ted, Ted, can't we do something?" Brysie cried out. "Where is that woman? We have to get Mark out of here."

There was another volley of rifle shots. It sounded much nearer; as if the troops had moved in. Then another, harsh and clattering. The muffled clamour of the rioters was not as steady now as it had been. Quite distinctly they could hear the sudden upsurges of confusion and panic.

"Ted," said Brysie, "Ted, can't we do something?"

She was still kneeling by Mark. Her arms were around him, holding him with great carefulness, as if he were some very fragile and precious object that might break if held too strongly. Mark could see the agitated flickering of her eyes as she looked at him. She turned her head and looked at Ted again.

"What are we going to do?" she asked.

The rifles sounded again, and on the echo of their sound they heard the sudden increase of human noise, disordered and with a note of despairing angry protest.

"I'm going out," said Ted. "Whatever you may say, Mark, I'm going out this time. I'll get someone to help me, and something to take you out on, if I have to take a door off the hinges."

He turned and went swiftly to the door. Mark watched him go and when his hand was on the doorknob gathered all the strength he had left and all the habit of discipline that had been established between him and Ted in their work.

"Goddammit, Ted," he said, "come back here." His voice was strong and hard with authority.

He watched Ted turn from the door, as he had known he would. He waited while he came back, slowly, a flush darkening the coppery skin across his cheekbones.

"Ted," Mark said, "don't do that again. You hear me? I don't want any dead heroes for the Party to-day. Heroes are all right, but not when they get messed up uselessly. They're only ridiculous then. I want to get out of here as badly as you, but we'll have to wait. You understand?"

"Yes," said Ted.

Mark tried not to feel too badly about it all. He knew that what he had done and the way he had done it had been quite necessary, but he hoped that the negative discomfort between him and Ted would pass quickly. It would be a sad ending if it didn't. Not tragic, but sad, when you thought of all the good things they had done together. And this part of it, the lying here waiting to die, this had not been the least part of the good things. Ted and Brysie had given it a dignity, no, not dignity, that wasn't the word. The old man had had dignity. Ted and Brysie had given it what? A distinction. Yes, that was it. Even if they

116

did not realize he was dying they had given a distinction, a distinction of tenderness and love to his end. It was more than he had a right to expect. He smiled up at Ted.

"Look, boy," he said. "You don't know how bad a riot is. It's . . . it's an explosion. It has to have destruction. Just pure destruction, without any plan. The people out there, the ones you'd have to pass through, they'll know by now the riot is over. That's going to make them angry. Before the troops get to them they're going to want something to leave a sign on. Buildings and the plate glass windows and burning motor-cars. But the most satisfactory would be somebody like you. You'd be the real stuff. Some of them might help you. But you'd be sure to meet the others, and nobody could help you then. A few might try, but not very hard. They wouldn't dare."

"O.K., Mark," Ted smiled back at him. "You're right. I won't try going out again. It was only that I felt I had to do something."

"What could have happened to that woman?" asked Brysie. "She *must* have got through to the police by this."

"Sure," Mark told her. "But there probably wasn't enough of them to come through."

It was so hot in the room that they were all sweating. Mark could see the greasy shine on Ted's face and Brysie's, and he could smell the stale odour from Brysie's armpits where her blouse had darkened with her sweat. He was cold and damp but for some reason he did not hurt as much as he had done. His mind felt detached and surprisingly clear. And this was one of the times that when he thought about dying he did not feel much fear. He only felt how much he loved Brysie, and wished he could find the words to tell her how she looked, close to him, and how important it was that he keep on seeing her face and having her arms around him.

"I wonder what G.K. is doing?" he murmured.

G.K. was the name by which the leader of the Party was known. He had come into Mark's mind as he lay there. The initials G.K. were for his Christian names, Gerald Keith. His surname was Hayes and he was a man who operated on a level Mark had envied and always known he could never emulate.

"I wonder," said Ted.

"He'll be in the middle of it," Brysie said. "He'll be in the middle of this somewhere. He'll be talking and even in a riot there'll be people listening to him, and maybe a few of them will go home when he tells them. It's a pity he couldn't be everywhere, they wouldn't need the police then, or the soldiers."

"I wonder what it is he has?" said Mark. He was not really talking to them. "I've watched him and thought about him and I still don't know. It's not only that he can speak, although he does that marvellously. It's something else. Something that the rest of us don't have. A power of engaging himself completely with the people so that they know it and trust it. He's the only man of my colour who has it naturally. The rest

118

of us have tried for it. Except you, Ted, you have it, and when you've used it for a while you'll have it like him. It's like being an artist, to have what G.K. has, so that everything you do and say about people comes from inside you and makes you and them one work."

2

There had been silence among them for a while in the room. Silence and heat. With the tart odour of uncured hot wood and the heavy smell of sweat and the ranker smell of drying blood. From the town they could still hear the riot; like a heavy swell of surf without the comfort or reassurance of the sea, and this sound broken occasionally by unexpected, always shocking, bursts of violent noise. That, they knew, was when something was destroyed. They had not heard the rifles again, but they waited for them when they would sound closer.

Ted was pacing slowly and nervously across the room, near to the window. Breaking his movements to look through the glass; sometimes he would glance across at Mark, or he and Brysie would exchange anxious glances. Brysie had become much calmer, or at least much stiller. Mark wondered if she knew how sad and ready for grief her face looked as she knelt beside him, holding his hand with her other arm on the pillow behind his head.

She feels it, he thought. She feels it, even if she isn't

ready to admit it yet. But she is beginning to feel what it's going to be. God, Brysie, I love you so much. My dear, gentle, tender, lovely Brysie, I love you so much. When I look at you I feel soft and almost desperate with wanting to know you more. Brysie, Brysie, Brysie, I love you.

"Jesus," Ted said at the window. "Why doesn't something happen. The lane is so damned empty. I can't see a soul; not a cat. Nothing except crows. It's like being on a desert island."

"It's like that in any war," Mark told him. "And a riot is just a very nasty sort of war. If you're not in the fighting you get the feeling of being lost and cut off from what's happening. You feel quite alone."

"I never want to feel as helpless as this again," Ted said. "Anything will be better than being trapped like this again."

"It's rugged," agreed Mark smiling at him. "It's not knowing what is happening and waiting for things to happen that's so bad."

"Mark," Brysie warned him gently. "Please don't talk. You'll make yourself worse if you talk. Just lie still. Ted, don't talk to him, please."

"I'm sorry," Ted told her. "I'll remember."

I wonder if I should tell her now? Mark asked himself. I'm getting very tired and I don't want to say much any more. I just want to lie here and feel tired without talking and try not to feel afraid of dying. Oh God, I'm tired. I wonder if I should tell her?

"Brysie," he said softly.

The Death

"Yes, darling?"

"Brysie, I love you. Put your cheek against me."

He felt her smooth skin, very warm against his, and she breathed deeply once.

"Mark," she whispered. "Mark. I love you so. Darling, I love you so much. We'll soon have you out of here."

She raised her head and looked at him. He did not think that he had ever seen anyone smile with so much sweetness as she was smiling now. He was very near to crying.

"Wait till I get you out of here," she said, very softly still. "I'm going to see you rest and rest till you're what you ought to be. If you don't take a holiday I'll beat you."

His tears had formed a hard lump in his throat. He swallowed and tried to accept the fact of what he was going to lose.

"I won't need the holiday, you know."

"Mark, don't be silly." She looked at him. Smiling with great fondness.

"Brysie! I mean I won't be here for that holiday. This damn business has got me. I'm really finished, Brysie."

He could feel the tears behind his lids. A huge sadness had filled his chest. He turned his head and put his face against the warm soft flesh of her inner forearm.

"It's happened, Brysie, and I don't want to die and not have you."

"No," she whispered. "No, Mark, no." Then, as he looked up, he could see her as she began to believe it.

"It isn't true," she said. "Mark, how can you know? Mark! Mark! You are not going to die. Mark, say it isn't true."

"I've felt it," he said, "for some time. But I'm sure now, Brysie. I know it's there."

And then she was crying. Crying quite quietly, without any of the spasms that often go with tears. She knelt beside the bed with the tears running down the sweaty shine of her cheeks, looking at him, and shaking her head slowly in a hopeless denial as she cried. And he saw Ted standing beside her, his face pinched and appalled as he realized what had happened in the time that he had been at the window.

Well, you certainly bitched that up, boy, Mark told himself. You gave it to her with a club. You could have done it different; made it easier. You know that. If you hadn't been afraid it wouldn't have been so damn clumsy, there wouldn't have been this sort of butchery. Anyway, you've been consistent. Right up to the end you've been consistent. You've bitched up and spoilt the people you wanted to love most, because always you were afraid of something. Afraid of what? This time it was dying. And the other times? I don't know. Having to really care about them, maybe. Having to love them so the consequences didn't matter. I was afraid of that, of having to give too much. Maybe that's it. And maybe it's the same thing as being afraid of dying.

The Death

Anyway it's lost you more than you would have had to give up. Lost you plenty. Your wife, for instance, and your son and what you had with them. I wonder what my son is like now. He was much boy even then. I would like to have had a son from Brysie; she would have made us a good son. . . .

3

He could remember how it had been living in London after the war, when he had been married to Jean and was studying for his first degree in law.

When he met Jean, it was the month they discharged him from the hospital, it had been like seeing in the distance the place you have been making for after a long and dangerous journey. And after he married her, for a while there, he had not been able to believe that anything could be so good and warm and so full of unexpected discovery. In a way it had been like being a child in a new delightful place, where every single thing you touch and feel and smell has a huge, uncontainable, chest-and-stomach-swelling significance.

They lived, in those days, in a square, white Regency house up in Hampstead. That is, they had the ground floor as a flat and the people who owned the house lived upstairs. It was a pretty good place to be living, and they had only got it because Jean's sister had married the son of the people upstairs.

It was near to the Heath, and in the afternoons when he came back from work Jean and he and Peter, their son, used to go out on to the heath. That was the time of day that Peter seemed to like best, out there on the edge of the grey-green, dipping and rising heath, with the hazy woods in the hollows and the prams and the handsome, thick-legged English girls playing hockey or walking their dogs. You hardly realized that you were really in a big city, although from the top of their road they could look down on the pearly gold of concealed London and the bell-jar of St. Paul's, standing out against the soft blurred edges of the other buildings.

In the evenings, after Peter had been put to bed, he and Jean ate big teas; sitting by the fire in the large yellow drawing-room which was hung with ancestral portraits and swords belonging to the people upstairs.

Before they were married Jean had said she couldn't cook. One time, in fact, they had gone walking in the Lake District with some other people and he had had to do all the cooking with another girl because no one else in the party seemed able to boil a potato.

But as soon as she got him to herself in a house Jean seemed to dig up a great deal of knowledge about cooking from somewhere. She used to make wonderful soup: taking a huge marrowbone as a base she would add vermicelli and diced vegetables and dried fruit and raisins and then simmer the whole thing slowly for hours. It came out like thick porridge and tasted better even than it smelt. He used to like that for tea, especially with those crescent-shaped, flaky, golden Aberdeen rolls that you couldn't chew like ordinary bread because they almost melted as you bit them. Jean had a friend in Scotland who used to send them down a box nearly every week. Even stale they were good to eat.

Sometimes after tea, when the curtains were drawn, and they were sitting on opposite sides of the fire, with the meal all digested and thickly warm in the blood, they would look at each other and something would move them exactly and irresistibly. Jean would come across to his chair and sprawl in his lap and they would, after a bit, roll off the chair on to the thick hearthrug with their clothes all disordered. And the coals burning in the grate beside them would sigh and hiss and crackle, and then fuse into a glowing crimson bank.

They were occupied and happy with love and with finding out a little more about each other every day and with helping their son out of being a baby into childhood.

There had been a lot of good friends in those first two years. At night the big yellow drawing-room, with its solid restful furniture, would be often full of the good friends they had.

Hancko and Bebler from the university. They had been in the war too and were going back to Czechoslovakia when they had finished their studies. Lorry Doran, the boy from Canada who had stayed in England because he liked it; Marion and Barbara, who were dancers and were both in love with Lorry Doran. There were others too, but these were the ones who used to come most often.

Hancko was the man that Mark liked best of all. Bebler was a good chap too, and Lorry Doran had suffered so much and so often during the war without it breaking him that he was almost a phenomenon; but Hancko and Mark became very good companions almost at once.

At nights when they were sitting round the fire, all of them, drinking the weak brown ale you had to put up with in England after the war, Hancko would do a lot of the talking. He talked well; and his thin ridged face, with the light blue eyes in their very clear whites, was an excellent vehicle for whatever he had to say. He had been in many situations and had felt them all accurately and clearly at the time; and when he was talking about them he always told them exactly as it had happened.

One evening he came home with Mark and they found that Jean and Peter had gone out somewhere to tea. It was while he was telling Mark about the time in Prague when he was hiding from the Fascists that he suddenly stopped and began to look at the photographs of Mark's family on the mantelpiece. Then he turned round and asked casually:

"Tell me, do you have any coloured blood?"

Mark recognized, with anger and embarrassment, the small halt in his breathing but he answered easily enough, "Of course. Why do you ask?"

"Shouldn't I? It seems an interesting point about a man like you."

"I suppose so," said Mark. "But it's not usual to hear a European ask it."

"It's an important thing," Hancko said. "Or don't you think so?"

"No," said Mark. "Yes. I don't know. I hadn't thought much about it."

"You have," Hancko told him. "You do still. It worries you quite a bit, eh?"

Mark grinned. It was a little wry and twisted but he made it a grin.

"Does it show so much?" he asked.

"You ought to have seen your face," Hancko said, "when I asked you."

"It's a queer business," said Mark. "Being my colour and my class in my sort of country. All your training . . . all your influences and most of the education you get encourages you to value one side of what you were born and to despise the other. It becomes a reflex by the time you're about five years old."

"What are you going to do?" Hancko asked him then.

"Do?"

"Yes. Do. What are you going to do when you get back? You must have thought of doing something with all those brains you have and all this legal training your grateful government is giving you free for patriotic services."

He was smiling, but Mark could see the hard, ridged

outlines of his face very clearly; and the light blue eyes, that were still a most definite blue in their extra-ordinary clear whites, were steady and not sharing in the smile. He's not serious, thought Mark, he's something more than serious. He's deadly. He's in a territory now where his confidence and courage in what he believes make him deadly.

"What I mean," continued Hancko, "is this. Are you going to be just a very good hack barrister? Or are you going to use what you have? Really use it?"

"I don't know," said Mark. "I don't know what it is I ought to do."

Hancko laughed. There was a definite note of relief in the laugh.

"I'm a bad guest," he said. "Forgive me. I just wanted to find out something."

"You're a son of a bitch," Mark told him. "Did you find out what you wanted?"

"Yes," Hancko said, and smiled. "Look, Mark, I talk a lot of politics to you. Why shouldn't I? Since I was fourteen my whole life has been politics. In the streets, at school, when I was working, in bars, in the concentration camps; anywhere I was, even in whorehouses, it was politics. For a man like me, and for one like you I think, there is only one way to move into life in our time. Only one way you can become a part of the life of the world and not something like a stone on it. You understand what I mean?"

"In a way," Mark replied. "That is, you and Bebler have taught me a lot, and I suppose the war must have taught me a little. I don't know enough yet, though."

Hancko had relaxed completely, lounging with one arm resting on the mantelpiece. With his ruddy clear skin and blue, light eyes he seemed curiously radiant. And the slender body under the cheap brown suit was compact and ready, like a naked rapier resting against a wall.

With a sense of astonishment, Mark suddenly realized that he could not guess Hancko's age. Over twenty-five and something under forty. But there were so few of those familiar signatures which, like the legend on a map, record the private story of one life. Nor could he have told to what class Hancko belonged. He seemed to have sweated away, in his work, all excess badges; fining down, now, to this intent, totally functional being. Not for another ten years, perhaps, would Hancko age. And then it would be sudden. Overnight, almost, he would show a decade's work and exhaustion.

He's something special all right, Mark told himself. There haven't been people of his type before our time. And there probably won't be that sort again. They're rather wonderful, terrifying and not quite human; and the way they've had to lose some of their humanity and the reasons for it, that's not just sad, it's inspiring, like tragedy.

"You asked me what I was going to do," he said to Hancko. "What were you getting at?"

Hancko moved away from the fireplace; he flung

himself into the armchair beside him with a precise, controlled movement, without heaviness.

"Everything," he replied, looking steadily at Mark, and with the accent of his English only discernible by the faint hardness of the vowels. "Everything you want to do, no matter how complex and untidy it looks, has something specific in it that moves the whole thing. An essence that you can get at." He closed his hand slowly, like a man grasping a sinking stone in the water before it reached the bottom. "Every question, comes down finally to 'What', not 'Why'. In our case it's a matter of giving an allegiance to the destiny of the poor. A real allegiance, I mean, that's almost like religious faith, but not quite. Don't mind that, though. It's an allegiance to them as a class, to what they have to offer, to the work you must do with them. In your country one lot of people who are white rule and prosper by using the people like you. They're able to use you because they allow you a good share in their world, and because they've given you a set of values to live by that depend on the approval of that world. And the poor of your world, the blacks, they're kept poor because you, people like you I mean, get an idea early in life that there will always be something irreconcilable between the white world and the black. And only the white world has any value, call it beauty if you like, for you. Is that right?"

"Yes," Mark said slowly. "I suppose that is the way it works."

"It's not a question," Hancko continued, "of

starting a race war: that's almost more stupid than the other thing. It's only a question of taking sides. Every time history becomes urgent and a little sick, as it is now, a man has to pick a side. Especially men like you who carry both your worlds within you, in your blood."

"Is that what you wanted to find out?" asked Mark.

"Yes. If you're neutral you're dead, in your situation. And if you make the other side use you, you're rotten goods. I just wanted to see what sort of man I'd made friends with."

They went into the kitchen then and made tea. They were very hungry and ate nearly half of a new cake that Jean had made. Then they went out and got quite drunk. You had to take a lot of beer to get drunk. Coming in later on they both wanted to piss so badly that they pissed in the garden. Jean had heard them stumbling up the path and came out to find them swaying about and spraying the lawn. She was very agitated and kept looking at the windows to see if the people upstairs were observing any of this. Both Mark and Hancko thought that possibility very funny.

That was how it had been those two years in London. And they had been the best two years he ever had.

Those were the years when he and Jean used to go up to Jean's mother and leave Peter there and take bicycles and go riding down the big, lush, almost too green West Country, or go over to Ireland. Once they had ridden down the valley of the Wye and found a place where they still made pear cider in the big stone

·troughs; the horse dragging the heavy stone crusher round and round the trough and the smell of the pears heavy in the air. Then when they had drunk they had ridden on till they came to a good place and he had spread his old gas cape and they had lain down and slept: and when they woke up they had rolled together and made love. They made love in the most inappropriate places on these trips. At least in places that would have been considered inappropriate to anyone watching.

At the end of these trips they could come up to London and spend the day with Hancko and Bebler, in the flat these two shared, before going up for Peter. And at nights they would go out and queue for theatre tickets; or they would go to the promenade concerts and laugh at the snobs who insisted on standing in the centre of the hall although they could get very good seats for about a shilling extra. Some people, they knew, really needed the extra shilling, but there were the others who wanted to show how much they could suffer for culture. Those were the ones they used to laugh at. They liked the music too.

Back at the flat, after the play or the concert, if Hancko and Bebler and Mark had all just got their quarterly grants, they would have laid in a few bottles of the cheaper red wine. They would drink these. Sometimes four o'clock in the morning would find them still drinking and singing. Or Jean would sing them Scottish folk songs. The real ones that make you want to cry happily even when you don't understand the Gaelic. Jean had a fine, thin, lost sort of voice that went very well with the songs she sang. Bebler had a guitar and he used to accompany her. Even when he didn't know the song she only had to give him the phrase and he was such a good musician that he could follow her, giving her the solid base on which to build the song. While they would listen, with the wine first cool in the mouth and then warm going down through the chest, the head light and that pleasant, faintly dead feeling you get in the mouth after you have drunk a lot of cheap wine.

All this was before the other women and quarrelling began. And before Hancko and Bebler went back to Czechoslovakia.

He never found out who told Jean about the big, broad-stomached, red-haired lecturer who had been at that students' conference he went to in Edinburgh. She had been a frank, sensual woman, with the full wide lips and the slight gap-tooth that many English women have when they are passionate. The second night of the conference they had gone for a walk in the big park. It had been a cool night and they had walked very briskly to get warm. And suddenly they had been excited, closely pressing, twisting on the ground, hands quickly grasping and clutching in a full, blind, never to be satisfied exploration. It had been very good and they had done it again every night till the conference ended, but it was never as rich and strange as it had been the first time.

He had gone back to London, though, with an

uneasy conscience. A presentiment that it was not going to end there. But it had been all right and he had almost forgotten about worrying when Jean found out.

He had never found out who told her. But someone had and after that the quarrelling and the suspicion, the making up that never quite made it whole and the suspicion again, destroyed the thing they had felt and built.

Then he had fallen in love, or thought he had, with Christine, the French student who came over to England on an exchange scholarship.

He had kept that from Jean until he found out that he had caught pox from Christine. He discovered this three days after he first went with her, and four nights later when Jean had wanted to go to bed early he had to tell her.

He had never forgotten the way she scrambled out of the bed with a twisted-mouth expression of disgust. And he had never forgotten her taut, loathing face as she leaned over and slapped him quickly, twice, so that his ears sang, saying as she did so, "You damn swine." It was the first time she had ever hit him and he had a smear of rage across his vision as he boxed her on the cheek. He did not sleep that night, but sat in the drawing room over the electric fire, listening to Jean as she cried behind the locked bedroom door.

When he got home next evening, Jean and his son were gone.

That was when the serious drinking had started.

The Death

When his money had nearly run out and they were thinking of throwing him out at the university for bad work.

Nor had he forgotten the morning when coming out of the flat where he had spent the night with a whore, he bought a paper to read on the bus going back to his flat. He had unfolded the paper and read what it had to say about Hancko and Beble. The arrest in Praguer and how they would be tried for a number of things he could not begin to understand.

It had been like that with him until one night in the pub near the docks. It had been a very silly sort of night, but it had been valuable because it was there that he made a moment of allegiance that would never let him go.

This night he was sitting at a corner table in the public bar with a girl he had got to know who went to bed if you bought her drinks.

He never noticed the two coloured boys with the overlong jackets and the too-small hats until one of the three sailors sitting at the table next to him said loudly:

"Cor, but those bastards get everywhere nowadays, don't they?"

"Too right, mate," one of the other two agreed. "You can't even give them a miss in your own country."

The first one saw Mark looking from him to the coloured boys. He became confidential. He leaned over.

"I tell you, mate," he said to Mark. "Give those bastards a chance and they'd be right in your home."

"Really?" said Mark.

"It's the flaming truth. You don't know those damn niggers."

"They don't seem to be troubling you or anybody," said Mark.

"Mate, you don't know niggers. I get 'em every trip down to Freetown. They all stowaway and come over here to marry white women."

"That's very interesting," said Mark.

"Tell you more, mate," the sailor leaned closer. A little closer, thought Mark, and I can hit him as I am getting up, without having to stand up to hit him. The sailor went on speaking, "You know what they come here for? To sell rope, you know, Mary Jane, the stuff; and to pimp for their bloody dark girls. Niggers. I'd like to send them back where they belong."

"Start with me, then," said Mark. "I'm a good nigger to start on," and he hit him as he got up. Bringing his fist from the waist, moving up and forward, body and arm and fist, with all the weight of his shoulder behind the blow.

And then, when he saw how fast the other two moved and felt the beer mug on his head, he realized that they would be too good for him. That he was going to get badly hurt. And as he went down, with the scream of his girl clear above the sudden confusion, he hoped they wouldn't use knives.

They kicked him pretty hard and as he rolled on

136

the floor trying to get under the table one of them
brought the edge of the heavy chair down on his head.

He had spent two months in hospital and when he
came out he had found that he didn't want to drink
any more and that he could work again.

That summer he had left England, and before he left
for Jamaica, he tried to get Jean back.

He had gone up to the market town in the Low-
lands where she had gone to live with her parents.
That day, as he started to walk from the station, it
began one of those misty, whispering drizzles which,
in summer, was one of the things he loved best about
this country. He had walked down the road with the
grey, granite houses gleaming from the rain, feeling
small and afraid. There had been a cool hollow in his
stomach and his heart had raced irregularly.

Jean's mother had opened the door and before he
could say anything she had shut it quickly, and he
was walking up the road to the station.

He had left England to go back to the home he had
not seen for eight years. . . .

4

"Brysie," Ted told her, "I'm going out. We've got
to get him out of here."

"Yes," she said. "Go on, Ted."

"No!" Mark tried to raise his head and gave up
when he found he was too tired. "Don't do it, Ted."

"Look, old chap," Ted said, bending over him and smiling. "Don't worry about me. I'll be all right, I'll be back before you know it."

There was too much tiredness to try and stop him. "Be careful," Mark said. "Do be careful, Ted boy."

"Sure."

Mark and Brysie watched him go to the door. He opened it, letting in a brief, shining glare, and then they heard his shoes on the concrete steps going down to the empty lane.

Brysie had her head on the pillow beside his. He could feel her arm as it lay lightly along his good side, and her cheek wet against his.

"Mark," she said. "You're going to be all right. They'll fix you up. You'll be all right. Wait and see."

The pain in his side, which had been constant but just bearable if he didn't think about it, came now as it had the first time. Drawing through him so he could feel himself shuddering around it and hear his staccato gasps. Stop now, he thought, stop now, Oh, Jesus Christ, stop now.

He was quite detached from Brysie and the room as he saw the incredibly ugly, malevolent figure of his death. It's coming, he thought, Oh God, it's coming. And then, with the worst of the pain, death went too and he knew that it had only showed itself but that it wasn't coming for him just yet.

He could feel Brysie tremble against him as she sensed the pain. Her fingers tightened a little on his good shoulder and she held her breath. But she said nothing.

You good girl, he told himself. Oh you bloody wonderful girl. What gave me someone like you? And I'd have kept you, too, if this hadn't happened. I wouldn't have thrown you away like the others.

"Ted shouldn't have gone." She was so close to him that it was no effort to speak. "I couldn't stop him, but he should have stayed."

"He'll be all right, darling," she told him. "He won't get hurt."

He knew she was wrong. But he was becoming more and more detached about what was happening around him. He could see things and yet he was getting too tired to feel them. It'll be my fault though, if Ted gets hurt. He'll be hurt because I didn't know what to do this morning when I got afraid. You never stop involving people in bad situations when you're afraid for yourself and what you might lose.

"Brysie," he said, "give me a little water. I don't know if I should, but give me a little for my mouth."

He watched her go over to the table and as she was picking up the mug they both heard the crashing roar of the rifles. It was very close.

For a long moment there was no sound but the drawn-out echo of rifle fire between buildings, and then they heard the people as they broke, over in the city.

It's odd, thought Mark, as he listened to the noise of dispersed confusion, it's very odd. When they were rioting you could only hear the swell of their voices, all sounding together. Now they're frightened you can pick out individual voices. Even at this distance. I wonder if that was the whole riot or only part of it? It's breaking through. It won't be long. The troops must have closed in on all the roads. Pushing them in to the centre and then breaking them off down the side streets. God, I hope they didn't kill anybody. They had both forgotten about his water as they listened to the babble and movement of the people breaking up over the city.

There was a sound of bare feet slapping on asphalt at the end of the lane. Brysie jumped to the window as the first of the mob came running. Their faces were sullen and abandoned. Their voices were broken and defeated. They called to each other as they ran. Some went into the houses and there was the sound of slamming doors. Across the road in one of the houses a child began to wail. It went on wailing and they heard a woman's voice full of angry fright and the sound of two ringing slaps. Down in the street some of the men had stopped and were talking in groups, standing tensely, their voices low and hurried. When another lot of the people ran into the end of the street they ran away too. Some jumped over the fences into the dusty yards. One man who had hurt his leg came down the lane in a staggering run. Trying to make the good leg do the work, hopping on the other leg. He looked very frightened. There were not many people in the lane now, but in a minute dozen a stragglers ran into it. They kept looking from side to side and two men turned into a yard. A door slammed behind them as they went into the house. The others kept on running and when they were under the window where Brysie was watching, one of them shouted, "Police come, oh! Police come!" They went on down to the end of the lane. Across the yard the child was still wailing. It wailed louder each time the mother slapped it.

He lay in the damp bed listening to the child wail and looking at the lithe, very strong curve of Brysie's back. Hearing, also, the sullen and abandoned sounds of the people as the troops fractured the sham cohesion of the riot.

He was thinking of the work he had hoped to do and how badly he had done that work.

It didn't start here, he thought. It wasn't only here I failed. It was a lot of smaller failures ending in this big one. Brysie was the first and only time I might have done something really well. And if I had had the time I might have done the other things well because of her. I might have learnt the business from the beginning and acquired the confidence that way. But I wonder where I went wrong? I wonder how I did it all so wrong that it had to end up like this? It beats me, all right. It beat the hell out of me. And I would like to have found out why. . . .

. . . When he came back to Jamaica he joined the People's Party as a matter of course. It was hard and confused going at first, getting used to his home again after eight years, the old man dying, and trying to establish himself as a lawyer in a place where there were too many lawyers. But in a while he found that things had arranged themselves around him and that he could try and do something for the Party and for the people who had put their trust in the Party.

He had regarded himself, at first, as a good lawyer who would use his training and be useful in the routine work. And that was how they had used him for a while.

Then they had asked him to speak one night at a meeting out in the country and that was where he found out what he could do with his voice.

He remembered how it had been that night; the big platform built of planks stretched across the empty oil drums; the kerosene flares around the platform twisting in the mountain breeze, each flame tipped with a curling feather of dark, oily smoke; the way the faces had looked around the platform, like one sculptured mass with the shining dark facets where the light caught individual faces, and the small dull glimmers of the eyes looking up at him; the sound truck parked in the shadows under the breadfruit tree.

He had intended to build his speech on the usual Party programme. But as he went on he found that a lot of the things he had learnt kept coming into the things you usually said in speeches like this. All the things he had learnt living with Jean, and watching his son grow up; what he had felt seeing Moira give him back his money that time in London during the war; how it had been that autumn up by the river, beyond Massachusetts Landing; and having to fight the sailors that night down by the West India Docks.

It had been difficult to speak of these things and he had not ever stated them explicitly. But he always knew when what he had learnt from these things came into what he was saying. He had been uncertain, at first, as to what he had learnt, but he found out as he spoke more. And the people had liked it. No doubt about that. He wasn't sure they understood it all: but then neither had he himself. He only tried to learn, and go on learning, as he spoke and wrote, after that.

It was during this time, when he was making the good speeches, and trying to find some way to feel truly and deeply what he talked about, that he had met Ted first, and then Brysie.

Ted was articled in one of the law offices down town, and he joined the Party when Mark was already an established figure in it. The two of them did some tedious and valuable work together and became known to the Party as a natural team.

One bye-election up in the country, they had held a meeting in the school-house and it was there he met Brysie. She had been one of the teachers and had come to hear him speak.

He remembered how, going back to town that night, driving out of the mountains, he and Ted in the car, he had talked about Brysie. He remembered that. And the next Sunday, going back to the place where she lived, and how she had smiled at him as he came on to the verandah, and the way he had spent that Sunday afternoon sitting in an old cane-work rocker talking to her father about the local politics, the crops, any number of things he had no intention of remembering while Brysie sat in a similar rocker at the other end of the verandah, sewing precisely, delicately, at a blouse; and how in the sometimes awkward pauses of his conversation with old Mr. Dean, Brysie's father, he would look up and catch her slight, ambiguous, confusing smile.

He had gone there several week-ends after that, racing his green Citroen out along the Spanish town road early on Sunday morning so that he would arrive in time for lunch. The days between each week-end he had worked with furious, concentrated energy, welcoming especially the dull routine stuff; going to bed at three in the morning, exhausted, to lie awake and think of Brysie.

With her, he had been so afraid of making one, irretrievable mistake that he had been almost clumsy. To touch her, to relieve his heart of its tight, restless burden of love by telling her, had been all that seemed really important to him. But he was afraid that if he tried this, even the cool amiable interest she showed to him would be destroyed. To have had her, in bed, at this time, would have been nothing. Everything he did, that time, everything he saw or heard or spoke, seemed strangely incomplete: as if his contact with the world was waiting on some tremendous resolution which depended on Brysie accepting his love.

144

The Death

Brysie taught him, in those first days, to read poetry. A thing he had not done much of before. She had in her small bedroom, in her father's neat, small-settler's house, a little beautiful bookcase of *lignum vitae*. It was very old and had been polished till the surface always seemed warm to the touch. Here, she kept the fifty or so books of poetry she had collected for half of her twenty-three years. Many were paperbacks, often without the cover, that had been given to her, or bought for sixpence when she was a girl; a few were stiff blue and gold, stamped with the school crest; and there were those she had bought for herself when she began to earn her own money. Sometimes, on those Sundays, she would read to Mark and her parents; and for the first time Mark had realized the enormous consequences of this art which was as questioning as music, yet somehow as hard and explicit as the Dutch paintings that he loved.

He remembered, also, the night of the debate. This had taken place at the old theatre in Kingston between himself and a man who had spent a long, destructive life selling, to the highest bidder, his marvellous talent for words. That night, he had gone to the theatre badly prepared, uncertain, knowing that he would do badly by the work and the Party. He had been angry and watched sullenly as the man he despised and envied got up to speak. But, as he listened, he had realized that he was being given his answer in the brilliant, intricate periods that were hypnotizing the audience and half-hypnotizing him. He had decided, then, to play the opposite. To speak only of the facts he had seen, in his own country and others, and he would do it with the greatest simplicity he could find. Without affectation, but deliberately, as a carefully staged contrast. When he rose, he had torn up his notes and flung them onto the floor with a precisely timed, theatrical gesture. But for all the acting, when he began to speak he had known that he was going to be better and more true than he had ever been. Not because of himself, but because of a combination of big and small circumstances he could not begin to understand, and which made this audience, in this place, at this time, demand such a confession.

He remembered that. And how, that night, as he was going out to his car with Ted, Brysie had come across the foyer of the theatre. He had stopped, staring, taken her hand and said foolishly, "Brysie! What are you doing here?"

"It's our half-term," she had said, "and I came down to hear you."

"Thank you, Brysie."

He had felt the words stumble awkwardly on his tongue and his heart was beating rapidly.

"It was wonderful," she had told him, then. "You can't know how good it was. I wanted to tell you that, so I waited. It wasn't you, really, it was what you believe in and the work you've done. That's why I liked it."

"Thank you, Brysie, thank you very much, that's about the nicest thing you could have said."

The Death

Her face, as she looked at him, had been naked, utterly serious, and suddenly the uneasiness and tension of the past weeks had gone, leaving a light warmth within him.

The next day, after court, he had driven her back home, although she had said she could take a bus. They reached her house, late in the evening, and she had said goodnight and got out of the car very quickly when he stopped outside her gate. She began walking up the little red-dirt path and he had waited and then said softly "Brysie." She had turned quickly and stood very still, with a pale, silver cloth of moonlight over her hair and face and shoulders. He had known, then, that there was only one thing he could say.

"Brysie, I love you. . . . I had to tell you that."

She had come back to the car, opened the door and got in beside him. She had taken his hand and said, softly, choosing the words carefully, "Thank you, Mark. I knew you did, last night. Please go on loving me because I think you are the nicest person I have ever met, and please keep on coming to see me because I want to love you as much as you love me before I say it." She had taken his face between her soft, dry hands and kissed him lightly on the mouth. Very lightly and softly, but he'd been able to re-live that delicate pressure on his lips all the way back to town. This was how it had begun. And a month after that, one Sunday, they were down at the sea. It was a shut-in, gritty beach, with only one tumbledown beach hut because few people cared to come to such an ugly little place. They had swum in the tepid, cloudy-green water and come out to lie in the sun. After a while, she had got up and walked heavily through the hot, loose sand, he sitting up to watch the lithe, smooth-backed figure, squinting a little against the powerful glare. She had called to him, soon after, from inside the hut, and he had got up and run across the sand, not expecting anything at all, only happy to have been called.

But when he bent his head to go through the low doorway of the rustling, coconut-frond hut, he saw that she had taken off her bathing suit and spread the big rug from the car on the warm sand. She was lying face downward on the rug with her head resting on her arms.

After that, she had come up to town, and he had given her a job in his office. He was making money then.

Everyone, of course, had talked, or rather whispered about it, and there had been some unpleasantness with his family. But what he had with Brysie he knew he was going to keep.

Almost right away it was as if they had known each other's flesh for years. Sometimes, watching her head on the pillows, moving from side to side, her face contorted and luminous with ecstasy, he felt strangely grateful.

He felt strangely grateful that he had been allowed to give so much pleasure to such a one as Brysie. . . .

148

"Brysie," he said.

"Yes, darling?" She came over quickly from the window.

"Nothing," he said. "Just Brysie."

Mark. Mark. My dearest. Please make him be all right. My lovely Mark.

5

Ted and the police came for them about fifteen minutes after the people had passed under the window.

They heard the deep hum of the station waggon engine before it turned into the lane; then the screech of tyres at the top of the lane as the waggon swung in fast and rocking over to one side. Brysie jumped up and ran to the door as it stopped outside. Ted was halfway up the steps when she opened the door.

"How is he?" he said.

"Bad. Thank God you've come."

A superintendent of police was getting out of the waggon. There were four black or brown policemen with him. One of them was pushing a folded up canvas stretcher through the door and another one outside the waggon was taking it.

All of them, the superintendent and the men with him, were pouring with sweat.

"I was almost up by the market," Ted told her, "when the people came by. They didn't even look at me. They were running too hard."

"I know," said Brysie. "Some of them came by here."

Voices Under the Window

The superintendent came up the steps. He was a fair-haired, very good-looking white Jamaican, although now his face was a boiled red and shiny with dried sweat. The men came up after him.

"I met the police soon after the people went by," Ted told her. "They were coming to Mark then. This is Superintendent Crawford."

"Nearly didn't stop," Crawford told him as he wiped his face with a filthy handkerchief. "I only recognized you at the last moment. How is he?" He jerked his head to the room and looked at Brysie.

"Bad."

"Let's get him out then. Come on, Matthews, bring that stretcher."

They all went inside.

Mark nodded and looked pleased when he saw Crawford. They had been to the same school, and they belonged, now, to the same cricket club. Crawford did not approve of Mark's politics and he would not have had Brysie in his home, but it's good, thought Mark, to see a face you know.

"Hi, feller," said Crawford. "Heard you got hurt."

"Got chopped," said Mark in a just perceptible voice.

"Filthy luck. Know who did it?"

Mark shook his head.

"Pity. We'll find him though. Come on, Matthews, get Mr. Lattimer out of here."

They all stood aside while the two men took the stretcher up beside the bed and held the edge of it a little below the edge of the bed. Two of the other policemen went to the foot and the head of the bed and another went between it and the wall. One of them drew back the cover and Brysie said, "Ah!" as they saw where Mark had bled on to the sheets. Crawford drew a breath back between his flattened lips. The three men lifted Mark easily off the bed and put him on the stretcher. One of them, the man at the foot of the bed, took the cover and put it round him as he lay on the canvas stretcher.

"Let's go," said Crawford. They all began to move to the door, the men carrying the stretcher going first.

"Crawford," said Mark.

Crawford came up quickly to the head of the stretcher.

"Yes, feller?"

"Did you have to kill anybody?"

Crawford looked down at him, his red face splattered with new beads of sweat, the trim, olive-green bush jacket wet and limp. Mark could smell the sun-hot leather of his holster. Crawford smiled gently.

"No, feller," he said, "not where I was. I came down by the race course and down East Street and across to King Street. It was pretty rough and we had to muss them up a bit, but we didn't have to do any killing. All the shooting you heard was high stuff."

"Thanks," said Mark.

"That's O.K.," said Crawford. He nodded for the stretcher carriers to move on.

You're a liar, thought Mark, as they carried him

down the steps. You're a liar, Crawford, but you're a damn fine policeman. You were lying to me back there about the killing because you know I'm dying. It's a good gesture, Crawford, old boy. But I hope to God you didn't kill too many, and I hope none of them were the women.

The driver of the police station waggon had taken out the back of the three rows of seats. They were piled up now in the space behind the last seat. They put the stretcher with Mark on it across the seats. It was a delicate business getting him in without jerking him too much, but when he was in it was comfortable and the leather smelt good and felt very warm.

With the stretcher in, there was only room for Crawford and the driver with Ted and Brysie. The others stood in the lane waiting for them to drive off. There was no one else in the street and they could feel the eyes watching them from the houses.

Crawford sat next to the driver, his back to the engine. Ted sat in the middle seat and Brysie was in the back nearest to Mark. She was holding his hand very tightly and looking at him. She hadn't taken her eyes off him since they left the room. He smiled at her, trying to close the distance that was growing between them.

"O.K.?" Crawford asked, leaning forward.

Mark nodded.

"Good. All right, Murray, fire away. Don't go too fast, though, I don't want him to start fresh bleeding." He leaned forward again.

The Death

"I'm taking you up through the back streets," he told Mark. "It's a little longer but the main roads are in a hell of a state. They won't be clear of all the mess they've scattered for hours."

"Brysie," Mark said.

She leaned over him to catch the words. The waggon was being well driven but the road was uneven and he could see her face swaying above his and her eyes red from crying.

"Ask Ted to come closer."

She touched Ted and pointed to Mark. Ted leaned over; Mark could see his face swaying as Brysie's had done, and the underside of the occasional tree branches which was all he could see of the outside, with the pale blue of the cloudless sky with the white glare on it.

"Hullo, boy," Ted said softly. "What's up?"

"Ask him," said Mark. "Ask him about the riot. I want to hear about that."

Ted nodded and smiled and pressed his good shoulder.

"Sure, boy," he said, still very softly. He sat up straight again. "What's it been like?" he asked Crawford. "How did it go out there? We've just listened. We didn't see a thing."

Crawford looked out of the window at the narrow empty lanes his driver was negotiating with such skill. He looked back at Ted.

"Pretty rotten," he said. "They've played hell and all. I don't think we've had anything as bad as this for quite a while. They've smashed everything they could smash and they looted. What they couldn't carry they dropped. You've no idea what the streets are like over in the centre of the town."

"Did you have much trouble breaking them up?"

"In places. One lot had got at a rum store. Must have broken into one of the bars. We had a lot of trouble with those."

That's where the killing happened, Mark told himself. Crawford's voice was not reaching him very clearly but he could hear if he tried hard enough. That's one of the places where there must have been killing. There were others too, Crawford, I saw it in your face back in the room. You're giving it to me easy because you know I don't want to hear it and I'm dying. You're a good lad, Crawford, in a stinking job.

The waggon stopped at a cross-roads and they saw and Mark heard the tracks of a Bren gun carrier clattering over the asphalt going towards the centre of the city. It was full of British soldiers. They were holding up a rioter who had taken a bad whiff of tear gas. His face was puffy and as the carrier went past them they could see the red slits of his eyes. A man was walking hurriedly and self-consciously down the street close to the wall of a shuttered Chinese grocery. When he saw the police waggon he stopped. They could see him trying to decide what to do. The waggon went across the road and turned up one of the narrower streets leading off it.

"Of course," Crawford said, "I was only in one

section, you know, and trying to get through to Lattimer. So I don't know what it was like all over. I pulled out as soon as we could get the waggon through without fighting."

"How did you know about Mark?" Ted asked him.

"They phoned through from the station by the market. Said a woman had brought the message. There were only two men there though, they couldn't leave."

"We wondered about the woman."

"She got to them evidently," said Crawford. "They'll be holding her for a statement."

He looked out of the window as the waggon made the last turn into the street that would bring them to the hospital. Further east, in the centre of the city, it was a good street, with offices and stores. Down here it was the sort of place where the rioters lived but in which the riot had not taken place. The houses were close together, leaning in dirty, dry-rotted, paint-peeling blocks. The coconut trees were stunted and the zinc was glistening white in the sun.

"Soon be there," said Crawford. "How are you, feller?" He leaned forward to look at Mark and straightened up. "Step on it," he muttered to the driver.

Brysie was holding Mark's hand, looking at him, passing her other hand constantly over his hair. Her breathing was rapid and shallow. Ted kept looking round at Mark and back at Crawford. Once Crawford shook his head almost imperceptibly at Ted and

tightened his lips. There was a huge silence and tense-
ness in the waggon. They could hear the shush-shush-
ing of the tyres on hot asphalt as they went up the
bright road to the hospital.

"Did anybody get hurt?" Ted asked Crawford in a
low voice. "Anybody from the stores and offices I
mean."

"Yes," Crawford whispered back. "Quite a few I
know of. They killed old Yakoub. We picked him up
outside his store in Orange Street. Stoned him down
when he was trying to get away with his daughter."

"Oh hell. What about the daughter?"

"The damnedest thing. They went for her of course,
but. . . ." Crawford looked at Brysie and his reddened
skin flushed deeper with embarrassment. He leaned
closer to Ted and whispered in his ear, finishing aloud,
on a note of amazement . . . "wouldn't touch her
when they found *that* out. The damnedest piece of
luck, eh?"

They were going very fast now, not worrying about
the bumping. They were passing more people now.
The streets were full of dazed-looking groups of people
standing around or hurrying with no apparent purpose.
There were police everywhere. Brysie had put her
hand under Mark's back to try and save him from
being jolted too much, and Ted was looking steadily
at his face. Mark tried to smile. Their faces looked
very huge now; so huge they seemed to fill the waggon.
He wanted to say something to them but he could not
remember what it was. Then the faces began to get

156

very small, retreating to an immense distance. He wanted to tell them to come back but when he tried to speak no words came. Someone was crying near him but he did not know who it was. He was very cold.

And, suddenly, he remembered what it was he had wanted to tell them. It came to him clear and he was telling them about it. But they were not listening. They were not listening at all and they were going further and further away. He had wanted to tell them that he had left the waggon. That he had gone outside into the white glare where it was hot and flat and endless. He was running now and his death was hunting him down. He was running, but in a heavy, tired way, lifting his knees high, and his death was coming in on his flank. It had headed him off and it was closing in and he was too tired to move ahead of that swift rushing flank attack.

He wanted to tell them that, but they had gone too far away. . . .

. . . That year, after the rains, he and Ted had gone into the mountains. They had gone far into the forest, beyond the Cuna-Cuna Pass, and camped out on the ridge under the cinchona trees.

In the mornings, when they came out of the tent, the mist had swirled in the ravine and they could hear the river moaning below the mist. Osbourne, the guide, would be boiling coffee and roasting sweet potatoes at the hissing damp wood fire, his long, incredibly seamed face shining from the flames.

Voices Under the Window

To get to the river they had to go down the ridge
through the long wet grass under the yellow cassias,
and then into the green mossy dark of the tree ferns
where the morning fog was still drifting. At the river
they couldn't see the ridge because of the mist and as
you waded out to the big rock the water was a dead,
iron cold. Under the rock there had been the small
jonga crayfish and they felt under the slippery green
of the rocks and pulled them off, putting them in the
gunny sacks. Then they would go up back to the ridge
and hang the gunny sacks in a tree so the dogs couldn't
reach them, and at nights Osbourne stewed the jongas
for supper.

They had followed all the trails that year: going
down into the damp, blue-green valleys or up across
the grassy, tree-scattered saddles to the forest of the
peaks. Up there the forest had spread, falling and
rising till it became blue and misty in the distance,
and the golden hawks had hung against the pale sky.

At nights the mountains had been sharp and flat,
with long clouds blowing across their faces. And when
they sat around the fire, the sounds of the river and
the noises from the forest came through a huge still-
ness. While the dogs, on the other side of the fire,
yelped and twitched in their sleep.

The dogs had found a thick, very clever old boar,
that year, as it was coming up from the river, and it
had led them three miles up the valley and over the
saddle between the two peaks before they surrounded
it in a grove of cedars. Mark had come up first, with

158

The Death

Ted and Osbourne still behind, jogging through the waist-high bush of the saddle. He had been so tired that his legs had nearly buckled as he unslung his rifle and had gone forward to where the dogs surrounded the huge, squealing boar; its flanks had been heaving and two dogs hung at the torn, bloody ears, their hind paws dancing on the leaves. When it saw him it had given a piercing defiant squeal and charged forward, the bristling mongrels scattering in the damp-smelling mould. It had killed one dog when they first surrounded it and he had seen the limp, ripped-open body as he fired, bringing the boar down. He had drawn the narrow machete and gone forward then, and bent down and slipped the point of the machete under the huge slab-like head into the soft throat and the tiny, unafraid, hating eyes had never left him and it had sawn madly at him with its tusks, trying to get up and charge even with the blade in its throat. When he pushed the blade in it had reared right up, its squeal cut short, but still trying to lower its head over the blade and with the dogs hanging at its ears. Even with his arm held stiff and the weight of the dogs on its ears it had almost reached his chest with the tip of its yellow, curved right tusk. And he had held it there while the blade went in and in, until he could feel the point grate on the vertebrae in the back of the neck and it had died, falling over on its side among the dogs. The blood had welled out around the blade and spurted on to his clothes and on to the damp, sweet-smelling earth of the valley. . . .

6

"He haemorrhaged," Doctor Rennie told them. "The bleeding would probably have been enough, but the haemorrhage finished him. It must have happened when you were bringing him here."

He was a stout, middle-aged, brown man with slack, unhealthy skin. He was smoking a cigar and had an expression of faint disgust on his face. This expression had nothing to do with his real character but was the result of twenty years' overwork and had been developed, carefully, during those twenty years.

Brysie was sitting in one of the two chairs that Rennie's office had. Ted stood by her with his hand on her shoulder. Crawford was standing by the window. They were all looking at Rennie who had come to the door and was leaning against the jamb.

"There was nothing we could do," he said.

"I would like to see him, please," Brysie said to Rennie. She spoke each word slowly and precisely. It was very painful to listen to.

"Yes, certainly," Rennie told her. "I'll take you up. We've put him in one of the private wards till his family send for him. Come this way."

Ted and Brysie followed him out of the door. Crawford stood by the window, leaning against the wall.

"I'll stay here," he said.

The three of them went along the dingy, grey-painted corridor past the wards. Rennie walked in front, his hands stuck in the pockets of the long white coat, the coat flapping about his short legs in their expensive grey tropicals, the neat ox-blood shoes twinkling. There was a smell of bandaged sores from the wards.

"In here," he said, turning into a room. Ted and Brysie went in after him. She was holding on to Ted's arm very tightly.

Rennie went over to the bed and twitched back the sheet. His disgusted expression was more pronounced than ever.

Brysie looked at the face of the man who had been her lover. It was inscrutable and unrewarding; like the faces of all the dead, except those who are terrified at the moment of death.

"Thank you," she said.

Rennie covered the face on the pillow again.

They went back along the dingy ward and the anti-septic odours of the corridor and into Rennie's office. Crawford was still standing by the window; leaning against the wall as they had left him.

"I'll take you home now," he said. "Unless you want to wait for Lattimer's mother. She's on her way down now. I 'phoned for her while you were away."

"No," said Brysie. "I don't think that would be a good idea. Take me home, please." She was holding on to Ted, her fingers hard round his arm. He could feel her trembling and her shallow rapid breathing.

Outside in the corridor she began to cry. She did not

cry as she had done back in the room above the lane, with the silent tears rolling down her face and no spasms. She had turned and she was clutching Ted, her face in his jacket. She was shaking so that he had to hold her very tightly.

"Ted," she was gasping. "Ted. Ted. Ted."

"You can take her back to my office," Rennie told him. "No hurry. Let her cry it off."

Ted put his arm across Brysie's heaving shoulders and led her back the few steps into Rennie's office. He shut the door behind them.

The two men leaned their backs against the wall and waited.

"She must have been properly in love with him, eh?" said Rennie.

"She must indeed," Crawford said. He took a cigarette case out of the breast pocket of his crumpled, sweaty bush jacket. He took out a cigarette and Rennie flicked him a light from a heavy, ugly lighter.

"You chaps have given me a lot of work to-day," he told Crawford. "You must have knocked them up quite a bit when you broke the riot."

"There'll be more coming," Crawford said.

"I'll bet on that," Rennie said.

The two men waited against the wall. A nurse passed them carrying an oddly-shaped enamel pan. Up the corridor a man in one of the wards started to call out loudly, "Lawd oh! Lawd oh! Lawd oh!" Crawford closed his eyes. He looked very tired. Rennie puffed his stub of cigar and squinted at him.

He did not look so disgusted now. He looked rather gentle.

"I wouldn't let it ride you," he told Crawford. "You'll just beat yourself out that way."

"I can't get used to it," Crawford said. "Every time it happens I tell myself it's just part of the job. And every time it happens it's the same damn thing."

"I know," Rennie said. "It takes a while to get used to it."

Behind the door Brysie was still crying. She was crying very loudly and they could hear her plainly.

It's only a black woman, Crawford thought, could cry like that.